What sounded like another shot whizzed past them. She inched over and peered out at the side mirror. A chain of headlights was speeding along after them. these people were all lunatics. Another shot seemed to miss them too.

Suddenly Jason began struggling with the wheel. "A flat! They must have hit a tire!" His next comment turned into a startled yell as the car suddenly veered sideways, bucked off the road, and began careening down the slope.

Aryl stared in openmouthed horror at the trees bouncing by them. Right in the path of their jolting headlights one very large tree was coming closer and closer. . . .

Also by Pamela F. Service:

WINTER OF MAGIC'S RETURN
A QUESTION OF DESTINY
WHEN THE NIGHT WIND HOWLS*
TOMORROW'S MAGIC
THE RELUCTANT GOD*
STINKER FROM SPACE*
VISION QUEST*
WIZARD OF WIND AND ROCK

*Published by Fawcett Books

UNDER ALIEN STARS

Pamela F. Service

FAWCETT JUNIPER • NEW YORK

VL 7 & up
RLI: IL 7 & up

A Fawcett Juniper Book
Published by Ballantine Books
Copyright © 1990 by Pamela F. Service

Library of Congress Catalog Card Number: 89-28025

ISBN 0-449-70404-1

This edition published by arrangement with Atheneum, an Imprint of Macmillan Publishing Company

Manufactured in the United States of America

First Ballantine Books Edition: December 1991

Some of this is for Karen,
and some for Gayle

✥ p r o l o g u e ✥

A THRILL OF FEAR AND EXCITEMENT TINGLED THROUGH THE
boy as he took up his station on the high redwood deck.
Dutifully he surveyed the houses and lawns below as evening settled over the comfortable suburban neighborhood.
Mothers had already called the younger children in, but
several older ones still scrambled after a soccer ball in the
deepening twilight.

The boy watched them, feeling deliciously superior.
Those kids were playing games, but *he* was carrying out an
important mission. He was standing watch, being sentinel
for the secret meeting.

This was the first Resisters meeting he'd been taken to,
and he was proud that his parents trusted him so much. Of
course, the other adults hadn't wanted him in on the actual
meeting where they planned things—the strikes, the attacks, the clandestine radio broadcasts, the pamphlet writ-
ing, and the rest. But it was important for someone to keep
guard as well. Strangers might approach the house or start
watching it, or a Tsorian ground car might cruise by. And
of course, it was important that he watch the sky.

Nervously he looked up. The pale evening blue was
darkening, and a few stars were beginning to appear—like

1

newly awakened eyes. He shuddered. Somehow when the stars were out, it did feel as if *they* were watching. After all, that was where they came from. The Tsorians, the conquerors of Earth. The enemy. Daringly he whispered the word aloud and felt a new thrill of defiance.

The enemy, yes, but they wouldn't win, they wouldn't be here long. Even after nine years, resistance hadn't crumbled. All over the planet there were Resister groups like this one. And someday their disruption, their sabotage, and their full-scale rebellion would work. The Tsorians would give up. They'd leave and let humans run their own world.

Again he scanned the neighborhood. The soccer game had dwindled down to two persistent players and one yappy dog. In the house opposite, a bedroom was lit up, and he could see a kid sprawled on the floor assembling a model. In another house, the fish-tank glow in the front room silhouetted a family watching TV.

Otherwise, though, there weren't many lights. The subdivision didn't even have streetlights. Good thing too, he thought, since it would probably foul up his night vision.

Again he scanned the sky. More stars now. He wondered how the old Greeks had come up with those crazy ideas for constellations. What patterns he did see didn't look anything like theirs. But then, they had probably spent a lot of time looking at the stars. They weren't afraid of them the way people were now.

A pity really, because those stars were rather pretty when you had to spend time looking at them like this. Some were set together like jewels, and some were big and on their own. They were different colors too. That one was almost red, and some of the others were sort of gold. And there was a blue one. Several. Blue. No!

He jumped from his chair in panic, staring at the growing blue lights. Then he jammed a hand down on the intercom. "Tsorians!" he yelled. "Blue ships! They're coming this way!"

The tinny voice on the other end was his father's. "Got you, Ricky. We're ditching. Get away from this house—fast!"

One more glance at the three blue lights, clearly closer now, and he dove through the door. As he pelted down the stairs, he heard slamming doors and yelling voices from the basement.

In moments he was outside. Like panicky bugs, Resisters were racing for their cars. The soccer players stopped their game and looked upward. Then, yelling, they began running for their homes. The squealing thrum of the ships already tainted the air.

He heard his parents calling him and began racing for their car. On both sides of the street doors opened and people stumbled out, looking up. Three glowing blue triangles were hovering above them. Screaming, people grabbed up little children and began running down the street, barely dodging the first fleeing cars.

He redoubled his speed, wishing his own car weren't so far down the street. Overhead, one of the triangles veered away, dropped, and flew low over the street. Blue energy shot from it. In an instant, the house they'd just left was engulfed in flame.

The air throbbed with it. Everywhere on streets and lawns, people, dogs, and cars fled in panic. Mouths were open, yet he could hear nothing but the ships and the flames.

His parents ahead of him. The car door open. Twisting, he looked back. The ship had turned and was making another run. Pulses of energy swept down the street, engulfing house after house.

The last thought Ricky Jensen had before the blue heat reached him was, "It isn't fair! The enemy shouldn't win."

✳ o n e ✳

THE PLANET HAD CIRCLED ITS SUN ONCE SINCE THE BOY'S death, but Aryl had been on this world's surface less than half of that time and knew nothing about it. Already she considered her stay far too long.

Standing now at the balustrade of the Headquarters plaza, she gazed out over the ocean. She frowned. It was wrong. The colors were wrong, the smell was wrong. Everything was wrong.

An ocean should be green, and so should the sky. And behind that sky, stars should stretch in a glittering curtain, close-packed and bright in their friendly familiar patterns. When *this* world turned from its sun, the sky was cold and dark with great stretches of emptiness between its stars. And those stars were all in the wrong patterns.

An orange disk sailed into her sight before curving back toward eager, outstretched hands. Turning, she stared at the native children laughing and playing at one side of the plaza. Suddenly her homesickness doubled. She was about the same chronological age as those children. Yet she was Tsorian. Last year she had gone through First Passage. The end of childhood. The end of playing and schooling and irresponsibility. She was bonded.

Sighing, she turned back to the alien sea. The sharp breeze battered her with its odd tangy smell and billowed the hair around her dark face into a pale gray cloud. Not that she could regret this change. It was the pattern of life. And her bonding was not an average one, because her parent was not an average Tsorian adult. She felt a comforting surge of pride. He was Rogav Jy, Commander of the Ninth Fleet of the Tsorian Empire. He was her father.

Below, the waves boomed and foamed over dark, green-splotched rocks. Their sound dulled the discordant strains of the wailing alien music. But at last Aryl turned from them and scanned the large mixed crowd, presumably enjoying the annual party that the Tsorian Occupation Headquarters threw for the native staff and their families. She picked out her father immediately. It wasn't difficult; his black body-suit and deep maroon complexion were the same as the other Tsorians', but his black cape was the only one showing a green lining, the color of command rank. The only one besides her own, of course, since as his bond-child she automatically shared his rank.

He was talking now with a native female, one with outrageous red-brown hair. Aryl tensed. Her bonding with her father was very close. She loved and respected him, and now bonded to him, she would complete her preparation for adulthood, for rank and career, under his training. She'd share all his activities and learn all that he assigned her to learn. But one thing that he expected her to learn still seemed highly distasteful—this mingling with natives and learning their ways.

Rogav Jy had an Empire-wide reputation for that sort of thing. They said it was something that helped make him a great commander, being able to understand aliens—friends, foes, or neutrals. But Aryl was only one year away from her sheltered nursery world. Aliens made her very uncomfortable, this batch particularly.

Just look at that female, she thought. Proper hair isn't red. It's black or white or a shade of grey; possibly ash gray like her own or a dark steel gray like her father's. But these people had an undisciplined riot of shades for hair, and for skin as well. Some were brown, some pink, some tan. Tsorians were orderly, uniform. From world to world, age to age, their skin was a calm, sensible maroon.

Aryl shook her head and looked away. The alien scenery was unsettling enough, but not as bad as the natives. Yet it seemed she couldn't avoid them. A young native male, with pale skin and hair a dusty yellow, now leaned against the railing not far from her. His attention was fixed where Aryl's had been a few seconds earlier, on the Tsorian commander talking with the native female. Aryl wasn't practiced in interpreting native expressions, but it did seem that this boy was scowling. She knew she'd have to force herself to talk with some native today, yet this one hardly looked like a promising target.

The boy abruptly turned his attention to the plate of food he was holding. He took a few jabs at something on it, then suddenly flung the whole thing, plate and all, over the railing. The brittle native crockery shattered, splattering food all over the rocks.

With raucous cries, a white, winged animal swooped from the sky and began gobbling the discarded morsels. Aryl shuddered, but the expression on the boy's face lightened. He reached into a pocket and brought out a chunk of some native food that he tore into bits and began flinging to the greedy animal. Within moments, two more creatures circled down from above and started squawking harshly and jostling the first.

Primitive and barbaric. Again Aryl shuddered and turned away. This whole world seemed so crude and uncivilized. How could these natives stand to interact so closely with animals, with grossly lower orders? She sighed resignedly. Well, if she was going to force herself to follow her father's example, she could probably find no greater challenge than talking to this surly, barbaric alien.

Jason glowered across the milling, jabbering crowd to where his mother stood talking with that alien. He was the one she'd mentioned, he supposed, the one with the green cape lining. Then, he recalled, had come another of her lectures, this one about how he should learn the Tsorian color ranking so he could tell one from another. But he didn't want to. He didn't care who was who. They were all nasty, murdering invaders as far as he was concerned.

And he certainly didn't want to be standing here watching his own mother talk with their chief! Angrily he turned back to watch the gulls gobble the food he'd flung to them. They were greedy and they were quarrelsome, but at least they were from Earth.

It was bad enough, Jason mused, having his mother be a known collaborator. What would the kids at school say if they knew he'd gone to this Tsorian garden party and munched their dainty hors d'oeuvres? Well, he admitted, probably most wouldn't care a lot. They thought more about the fortunes of their school teams than about their planet having been gobbled up by an alien empire. But the kids he cared about, the ones he wanted to get in with, they'd think coming here was next to treason. Some of them, after all, had actually been friends of Ricky Jensen's.

Jason had known him too, but not well. Ricky had hung around with those other kids, the ones who furtively called themselves Resisters. And none of them would have anything to do with Jason—not with the son of a collaborator.

Later, of course, they'd all learned that Ricky's parents had actually been Resisters, real ones, and they'd belonged to a secret group. But it hadn't been quite secret enough. Last year the Tsorians had wiped it out, along with Ricky and half a neighborhood. It wasn't far from home, just over the hills, and Jason's mother had taken him there once to see the devastation. The Tsorians didn't let such spots be built on again. They wanted them to remain as stark reminders of the consequences of defying the Tsorian occupation. But to Jason it had seemed more a reminder of why that occupation needed defying.

The food splattered over the rocks finally ran out, and the seabirds flapped heavily off in search of other pickings. Reluctantly Jason turned back to the party.

To his surprise, a Tsorian was standing nearby, a young female looking right at him. At least he thought she was young, though her hair was almost white. Stupid to have drab hair colors that didn't even give a clue to a person's age.

Jason was turning back toward the ocean when the girl took a step closer and spoke in dry, harshly accented English.

"I see you have provided your own entertainment, feeding those . . . animals. Amusing, but don't you want to throw disks with the others?"

"I don't feel like playing."

"Oh. Do you come here to the Headquarters often?"

"No, not if I can help it."

She was silent a moment, then said, "It is beautiful here."

"It was," he began, then continued boldly, "before you

Tsorians came. My father used to tell me there was a park here by the water. With the redwoods and Mount Tamalpais beyond, it probably *was* beautiful."

The Tsorian frowned. "Come now, this planet has more than enough wilderness. It's almost unkempt. Our Headquarters doesn't intrude on you."

"Intrude? I suppose wiping out armies and rebellions and innocent civilians isn't intruding?"

"We can't let you natives disrupt our holdings here. This is a strategic planet. The needs of the Empire must come before those of a few natives."

Quivering with anger, Jason looked straight into her pupil-less eyes. Eyes like black marbles, he thought, like hamsters' eyes. "Have you any idea how arrogant you sound, calling us 'natives' as if we were a pack of primitive Indians?"

The other breathed in sharply and flexed her claws a moment as if contemplating some violent response. Then she shifted her gaze beyond him, across the Golden Gate Bridge to where the city of San Francisco gleamed in the afternoon sun.

"Indeed," she said simply. "And who are these 'Indians'?"

"The people who lived here before the Europeans came and took over."

"And these 'Europeans' had a superior technology?"

"Of course."

She smiled tautly. "So there it is, the natural order of things. You see, it really is just the same."

Jason grabbed the railing to keep himself from sending a fist through that sneering alien face. "It's not the same at all! The Indians and Europeans were one species. Sure, they squabbled about land, but you Tsorians came and took everything from us, from all of us, Indians, Europeans, everybody. You took our independence, our future!"

"Ridiculous! We've given you a better future."

"Oh, really? The only marvelous technology you've shared with us is the business end of your weapons!"

Jason turned and snatched a plate from the automatic serving tray that was gliding by them. One by one he picked the glistening curls of meat off the plate and tossed them onto the rocks. Cheering raucously, two sea gulls swooped from the sky and began fighting and gobbling. The Tsorian glared at him a moment, then abruptly turned and stalked away.

Jason smiled grimly and continued to watch the gulls. At last he'd said what he'd wanted to say. And he'd said it to one of *them.*

Slowly his elation faded. Big courageous act. Gripping the plate, he launched it like a Frisbee onto the rocks, scattering the startled birds. Someday he'd *do* something, something besides talk. Something that made a difference. Ricky Jensen had tried, hadn't he? Well, someday he, Jason Sikes, would try too. Only he'd succeed!

❖ two ❖

ARYL STOMPED AWAY. WERE ALL NATIVES THAT RUDE AND obnoxious? Probably not or they wouldn't be working here in Occupation Administration. And besides, these aliens did things oddly. Young people didn't bond with a parent, didn't work with them in their careers. That boy's parent probably wasn't anything like him. Still, it was hard to imagine such incredible disharmony between parent and child, alien or not.

Well, she wouldn't try. This compulsory event was unpleasant enough without dwelling on one misfit native. She looked around, then joined a group of young Tsorians. They saluted the command green of her cape and began speaking with guarded respect. Bonded to parents in Fleet or Occupation forces, they too were bound by protocols of rank. As long as their capes all bore the same rank-color, they could talk and joke freely among themselves, but with her they had to be respectful.

Aryl left them as soon as politeness allowed. Not a whole lot more pleasant than her last encounter, she had to admit. She could almost see why her father mingled with natives, sympathetic ones at least. Relations with them were outside restrictions of protocol, while every

Tsorian here, besides herself, was below his rank and strictly not to be fraternized with, outside of duty.

She looked about for him now. He was no longer with that native woman but was standing near the exit. Good. Maybe they would soon be going. Aryl made her way through the crowd, then slowed as she saw that her father was talking with Oimog Vak, Governor of the Occupation.

Governor Oimog's hair was a lighter gray than the Commander's and she was nearly as tall, but under her standard tight black uniform, her body was going to fat. Rogav's was solid and muscular, and at the moment, Aryl noticed, it was tense with anger.

Aryl moved within hearing. Whatever was her father's business was hers as well.

"Commander Rogav," the Governor said in an oily, unpleasant tone, "I won't be put off any longer. I need those ships."

"You wouldn't need them, Governor, were this occupation being properly run."

"It is being properly run, Commander! Precisely by the regulations. This is no Colony, let me point out, nor even a Ward World. It is an Occupied Strategic Planet. Occupied for the sole purpose of providing the Empire with a foothold in an endangered region."

The Fleet Commander showed his pointed teeth in a calm, humorless smile. "I do not dispute that, Governor, nor do I doubt that you are running things strictly by the regulations. What I dispute is the adequacy of those regulations. Since each world and each species is different, logic dictates that each set of occupation regulations should be different. If the Hykzoi can be kept at bay, this world will eventually be upgraded in status. Instead of occupied

13

aliens, these people will become colonials, a regular part of the Empire. Why embitter them now?"

Oimog's sneer was poorly concealed. "Your reputation for being soft on aliens precedes you, Commander. It may win you some sort of romantic maverick status among your troops, but it will have no impact here. I have final say on how this occupation is run, and I will not cede it to a military troublemaker with a tenuous political future."

Aryl was appalled to hear anyone speak to her father like that, although she knew the Governor, being outside the military hierarchy, had a limited right to do so. But her father only shrugged.

"Not a totally inaccurate description, I admit. But may I point out that I am also a Fleet Commander—in your sector."

The Governor sniffed. "That is condemnation in itself. This isn't a bad occupation assignment, but for the military it is clearly a dead end. I have learned where you stand politically. Those who sent you here were looking for somewhere to dump you—a region technically endangered but where there was little likelihood of trouble *actually* happening or of your making more of a name for yourself."

Indignantly Aryl stepped to her father's side, though as was proper, Oimog took no notice of her as a separate individual.

Rogav plucked a drink off a passing serving tray, balancing the goblet delicately between his three clawed fingers. "Again, not a bad analysis, Governor, except for one thing. In my estimation, and I am not totally alone in this, trouble is *extremely* likely to happen here. True, a single fleet is a modest force, but the Empire has demands on many borders. And not everyone is as devious or as militarily blind as certain occupation governors or their friends. Fleets are not sent around the universe solely to advance or squelch a single political career." He took a slow sip of his drink, then continued, "With proper leadership, a fleet stationed here could hold back a Hykzoi attack. It could, that is, if that fleet were not depleted by inept governors trying to hold together poorly run occupations."

Oimog Vak opened and closed her mouth several times, then abruptly she turned and strode away.

Rogav chuckled into the remains of his drink. "Well, Daughter, now you see why I have such a 'tenuous political future,' as Oimog so aptly put it. I just can't keep from pointing out uninformed, pompous fools."

"Well," Aryl said, "at least she won't get your ships for her occupation."

Rogav sighed, his dark, craggy face taking on new shadows. "Ah, but she will. Strictly 'by the regulations' occupation governors do have the right to demand support if the military force is not on combat alert. I'm already in quite enough trouble with some Imperial authorities without being accused of contributing to the failure of an occupation. Never mind that it's the heavy-handed occupation tactics that are causing that failure. I know her political connections won her this post; they're far better than mine will ever be. But even a bureaucratic blockhead like Oimog ought to see that these natives need to be dealt with differently."

As far as Aryl was concerned, she'd as soon they weren't dealt with at all. But at least the matter was only a peripheral one for her father. The Hykzoi threat was the reason the fleet had so recently been sent here. And the suggestion that an actual confrontation might be more imminent than they'd thought—that was exciting. The sooner she got off this planet and saw the sort of action she was being trained for, the happier she'd be.

Jason stared out the car window, but his anger kept him from seeing much. The bridge girders swept by as the car sped eastward across the Bay.

His mother finally broke the heavy silence. "Well, now you see, Jason, that wasn't as bad as you thought it was going to be."

"No, it was worse."

"Oh, come on. I saw you talking with that girl, the Commander's daughter, judging by the green cape."

"I don't care whose daughter she is, she's an arrogant creep. She started the conversation, and I stopped it." For the first time since they'd left the party, he turned to look at his mother. "But I did see you in what looked like a long, happy talk with her scumbag father."

"Jason! Rogav Jy is the most important Tsorian on this planet."

"Mother, he's one of *them*! Our conquerors, the enemy. What have they given us in exchange for making us all slaves? A few Headquarters jobs and an annual garden party!"

His mother shot him a strong, sharp look. Not anger so much as something Jason couldn't quite define. Then she jerked her attention back to the road.

"I'd hardly say we are slaves, Jason. The Tsorians may have readjusted things on the national and international levels, but they've scarcely interfered with the economy or local governments or the education system—not with anything really important."

"So, humiliating our armies and dictating to national governments isn't important? Or what about incinerating

16

those private radio transmitters, or crushing those rebellions in Australia or Pakistan or Denmark? Or, how about what happened over in Walnut Creek last year? I suppose having their neighborhood wiped out wasn't really important to those people."

Marilyn Sikes frowned, then answered tensely, "Those people brought it on themselves. And remember, the Tsorians have only been here ten years. There's bound to be trouble at first."

"Not just at first, Mother. Some people will never give up. Not everyone's as easy to beat into submission as you collaborators."

For a moment, the only sound in the car was the steady rumbling of tires. Then his mother said in a taut voice, "Jason Sikes, I am not a collaborator. I am a realist, and I should also point out that I am your mother. I won't have you talking to me like that."

"Then why don't you start acting like a mother I can be proud of?"

Abruptly he turned back to the window. The lights spangling over the dark East Bay hills blurred and shimmered. He swallowed and blinked, but refused to be seen raising a hand to wipe away tears.

That's what he really wanted, he realized suddenly, someone to be proud of. Ricky Jensen had had that. It was a ghastly way to go, but at least Ricky and his parents had been together, and he hadn't been ashamed of them.

Even that nasty Tsorian girl, Jason supposed, probably was proud of her father. She had certainly been loyally spouting their propaganda.

Jason clenched his fists. How sick can you get? Here he was actually envying a dead boy and an arrogant alien girl. He scowled at the lights and the crouching darkness.

17

❈ t h r e e ❈

BRILLIANT PINPOINTS OF LIGHT UNDIMMED BY ATMOSPHERE, the stars receded endlessly in all directions. Aryl hung suspended in a void. She gripped the arms of her chair, trying to maintain some sense of up and down. Suddenly the vision blurred and shifted. A new stellar pattern emerged, dominated by a single bluish star circled by tiny flecks of reflected light. Aryl felt immensely sick.

"The Ydrog System, sir." First Adjutant Theelk's sharp voice jarred in the darkness.

"And the Hykzoi bases there?" Aryl heard her father speak from the void beside her though she could see nothing but stars. In response to his request, the focus zoomed in on the planetary systems. Again Aryl's stomach lurched. She had been looking forward to her first trimensional briefing. Now all she could think about was not disgracing herself by getting sick.

Theelk's crisp response burst out of nowhere. "Our probes have shown increased activity where the flashing lights indicate. However, this may be due to massive retaliation for a rebellion on the innermost planet."

"And the status of the rebellion?" Rogav asked.

"The Hykzoi largely obliterated the native population, sir."

"Hmm. Typically Hykzoi. And from our point of view, at least, very helpful."

From somewhere to Aryl's left Subcommander Hlon Az piped up, "How is that, sir?" Aryl was relieved. She had wanted to ask that question, but didn't trust what her digestive system would do if she opened her mouth.

Her father answered. "The native population of Ydrog's innermost planet was a major source of slave labor for Hykzoi projects in that sector. If the Hykzoi were willing to eliminate them, then it's safe to assume that this sector is not the location of any Hykzoi military buildup. So we may look elsewhere for the origin of a Hykzoi attack. Now, Theelk, anything from the Oanu probes?"

Aryl braced herself. It was the sudden sweeping changes that were the worst. She wished she could close her eyes, but didn't dare risk missing any of the briefing because her father might quiz her on it.

As the universe resettled, Theelk replied, "Nothing, sir, but the Ih Erzu probes have reported undefined activity just beyond the range of effective detection. Somewhere here, in the direction of the Qvi-Nars Corridor."

"Hmm. It could mean a new farming complex as easily as a military buildup. But in the absence of anything more solid, it is something. Now, Theelk, switch to the two-empire overview."

Aryl dug her claws into the chair, but that did little to steady her stomach as the scale plummeted. Hundreds of stars became thousands. Overlain on the starfields were two transparent clouds of color, red and blue, spreading toward each other.

"Finer," the Commander ordered. A pulsing change, and a magnified portion of the blue stain was shown protruding into the red.

19

"That, Subcommander Hlon, is the trimension we'll use in tomorrow's briefing of the strike leaders. They must remember that this is a beachhead for the Empire and a very tenuous one at that. I believe that the Hykzoi, at least, are fully aware of this, and that far sooner than some elements seem to realize we will be facing a substantial Hykzoi attack. Since I can't seem to convince the authorities to strengthen our forces here, we'll just have to be alert and do our best with what we have."

Hlon's voice quavered slightly. "Then in deploying our forces, the positioning of our vanguard could be critical."

"Correct. And that is precisely the purpose of this exercise. We must pinpoint the origin of that attack before it is launched." Gratefully Aryl heard her father stand up. "That will be all for now, Theelk."

Instantly darkness vanished, and the universe shrank to the confines of a single office. Aryl's black eyes blinked rapidly as she tried to adjust to the welcome flood of light through the now-transparent walls. Still not trusting her stomach, she let her father escort Theelk and Hlon to the door.

When he returned, Rogav stood looking at her severely a moment, then smiled broadly. "Well, Daughter, I'm proud of you. At my first trimensional briefing I got sick all over my captain's boots. You'll get used to it, though, and there're some mental tricks I can teach you to help with those sudden transitions. So, anyway, what did you think?"

"About the content of the briefing?" Cautiously Aryl stood up and walked across the room to the curved transparency of the wall. "I think we'll be stuck here a while longer until the Hykzoi either begin their attack or we figure out where it's coming from."

Her father sighed. "Correct. And I am not a patient person; I don't like waiting." He joined her and together they looked across the narrow channel of choppy water at the odd angular towers of the native city.

"I particularly don't like waiting on a newly conquered world. Not one that's been conquered in this manner, anyway, as an outpost rather than a colony. The natives are always obsessed with what they've lost and still don't realize what they stand to gain. This group, I think, has particular promise. They're quite spunky, really, and there's much they could offer our philosophers and artists. Oimog's a fool to treat them as she does." Rogav laughed ruefully, then added, "And I must confess to a certain reprehensible prejudice for species that basically resemble my own. There are few enough of them in the universe as it is."

Feeling Aryl shudder, he chuckled. "But then I forget, this is your first alien world. On my first one, the natives resembled blobs of turquoise jelly. They were quite clever, but kind of hard to relate to."

Aryl frowned, trying to imagine talking with creatures like that. She failed. Her father continued musingly, "You know, if I live long enough to retire from the military, I think I'll go into education. They really ought to introduce more alien species onto the nursery worlds. Too many children go through First Passage without knowing a thing about them."

"But that's the sort of thing bonding is for."

"Hmm. I suppose you're right. There really wouldn't be much point in a kid bonded to a clerk on Yaxil Majhat learning all about flying amphibians or turquoise jelly blobs." His voice turned serious again. "But for someone bonded to a Fleet Commander, there's a lot of point in it. And this is a good enough group to start with."

Aryl looked across to the alien city. Already she and her father had walked its streets and visited its museums and places of recreation. The natives had things they defined as art and music and architecture, but she had trouble seeing them as such. She could probably manage to if she tried. But frankly, she didn't want to. She just wished the Hykzoi would hurry up and attack.

Rogav turned away and strolled back to his desk. "I've decided that what we need now is something more intimate than tourism and academic study. I'm inviting a couple of natives to have dinner with us. That's the get-acquainted custom here. The adult is a female who works in the Headquarters liaison department. She has a son about your own age, so that should be interesting for you."

Interesting! Aryl's stomach churned. This could be worse than a trimensional briefing.

"Mother! How could you?" Jason jumped up from the dinner table, sending his chair careening back against the sideboard.

"Jason, sit down," Marilyn Sikes said patiently. "Think about it. It's like he's my boss. I had to accept a dinner invitation."

Jason righted his chair and dropped angrily into it. "You make it sound like you work for some insurance company. Mom, he's a conquering monster!"

She reached across the table and firmly grabbed her son's hand. "Not a monster, Jason, a Tsorian. But the conquering part is right. His people conquered ours ten years ago. That's something we have to accept."

"My father never accepted it!"

Briefly her face crinkled with pain. "Your father died seven years ago. A lot has changed since then."

"Yeah, but not for the better."

"Maybe not, but that doesn't change the reality of it. And present reality is that Fleet Commander Rogav Jy has invited us to dinner, and we will accept the invitation."

Jason snatched his hand away. "*We* will not. Go ahead and pander to that monster if you want, but count me out!"

Jumping up, he rushed to the front door, then turned and looked back at his mother, his face red and crumpled. "When I was little, I used to think you were wonderful. You and Dad could do nothing wrong. Then Dad died, and you took that awful job with them. And now you're a traitor, and I don't want anything to do with you!"

He slammed the door behind him. In the chill night air, his tear-dampened cheeks felt clammy and cold. Angrily he rubbed them, but tears kept welling up, blurring his vision as he ran. Yet he hardly needed to see where he was going. He knew.

Indian Rock. Always his special place, his refuge when he needed a world of his own. At the end of his street it rose up, a huge protrusion of bedrock and tumbled boulders with houses lapping all around its base. In its crags and crevasses, caves and cliffs, were places for hiding or for games or for quiet thinking.

It was thinking he needed now, that and solitude. Heedless of any danger, he scrambled up the steep, rough stairs, little more than hollows in the stone, supposedly made by Indians who had once used this place. Finally he levered himself onto the broad thronelike boulder that crowned it all and sat hugging his knees, tensely looking about him.

His eyes had dried, but his throat and chest still knotted

with misery. The cold wasn't bad, although in the west, the fog had already spilled in from the ocean and covered the Bay. The lights of San Francisco were lost under its pale shroud, but around him the Berkeley Hills still sparkled, and above, the stars shown clear and untroubled.

Untroubled? Hardly, he thought bitterly. They were where all the trouble came from. There was nothing comforting or friendly about them.

When he was very little, his dad had taken him out here to look at stars, and in the summer they'd gone out on the beach at Uncle Carl's cabin. Dad had told stories about the constellations, the Greek ones and the Indian ones, and sometimes too he'd told stories about what it would be like when people finally went out there, the adventures they'd have in space and the discoveries they'd make. Jason had loved it all.

Then came the night when the sky had flamed with explosions as their air force shattered under the Tsorian invasion. After that, no starry sky had seemed the same.

Jason's father had never forgiven the Tsorians for that or for anything else. It was more than just taking the stars from us, he used to say, it was betraying our past and stealing our future. Jason had not really understood that then. Now he did.

Jason cradled his head on his knees. Now he felt the same about himself—betrayed past, stolen future. Agreed, his mom had needed a job after his father was killed in that plane crash, but why did she have to take one with the Tsorians? Didn't she care anything for her husband's beliefs—or for her son's?

He lifted his head, but the stars were gone, blotted out by the rising fog. Good. The fog was cold and dank, but at least it came from Earth.

After a while, though, it was too much, chilling his skin and seeping into his bones. Stiffly he lowered himself off the top rock. He'd have to go home now. But he wouldn't stay. If he'd made any decision tonight, he guessed that was it. He'd have to leave home. Maybe he could stay with a friend or with Uncle Carl. Or maybe he'd just drop out of school and get a job and live on his own. He couldn't keep living with his mother, not anymore, not the way she'd become.

His decision was made, but it didn't make him feel better. As he began working his way down off the rocks, it hung in his chest like something heavy and cold. Standing at last on the pebbly ground, he noticed that the fog seemed thicker. In it, the twisted branches of a nearby oak looked strange and menacing. Beyond, tall blurred shapes of eucalyptus loomed like disembodied ghosts. The only thing visible beyond that was the eerie yellow smudge of a streetlight.

He started walking toward the light, then stopped. A new shape was taking form in the mist, taking form and moving toward him. A voice came, flat and muffled. "Jason, is that you?"

Instantly he was angry at himself for feeling relieved. "Yes, Mother, it's me. What do you want?"

"I want you to come with me someplace tonight."

"No, Mother, I'm not going. I'm not going anywhere with you, not anymore."

"Jason, please. Don't argue. Just get in the car. I've brought it here."

"Mom, it's no good. I'm not going—"

"I said don't argue! Jason, please just come with me tonight. All these years I've tried to protect you. I should

25

have known it wouldn't work. You're too much like your father."

Jason opened his mouth to protest again, but his mother raised a hand. "No, Jason, please. If you still want to argue, we can do it later. But there's a meeting I've got to go to, and I want you to come along. Don't worry, it's not another Tsorian garden party."

Suddenly Jason was very tired. He didn't want to argue. The sight of their old Chevy glowing bright and green in the fog was comfortingly familiar. He'd go along with his mother just one more time. Tomorrow was soon enough to make the break.

They drove in silence along fog-dimmed streets. Trees and mailboxes seemed to float in front of nearly invisible houses. The fog became even thicker where the hills flattened and spread westward toward the Bay.

Jason didn't want to think, let alone talk, but his mother finally spoke up. "There's one thing you need to know, Jason, even before we get there. It's about your father."

Jason stiffened. If she said one carping word about his father being an idealist or anything, he'd jump out of the car at the next stop sign.

"You know how he died?" she asked.

"Of course. In a plane crash up north."

"That's what I've always told you, but it's not true. He *was* booked on that plane, and it did have mechanical troubles and crash. But he never got on it. He was killed the day before, the day the Tsorians put down the Seattle Uprising. Your father was one of the Resister organizers there."

Jason leaned back against the seat. He felt very odd, as if someone had just reached inside his mind and rearranged the pieces. He tried to see the new picture but couldn't focus on it.

Suddenly he turned to his mother, frowning. One portion had emerged. "Then . . . then if Dad was a Resister, if he was actually killed by the Tsorians, how . . . how could you have done this? How could you have turned collaborator and actually gone to work for those murderers?"

"That's the other part of what I'm trying to tell you, Jason. I'm a Resister too, I always have been. It's a Resister meeting we're going to tonight."

▓ f o u r ▓

JASON DIDN'T HAVE TIME TO LET THIS SECOND REVELATION do more than jiggle at his mind. The car slowed, then swung through an open gate in a chain link fence.

For blocks they'd been driving down wide, deserted streets past yellow smears of streetlights and drab bayside warehouses. Now he stared at the similar, fog-obscured building before him. No windows, no signs, weeds dotting the cracked and littered parking lot. They rounded a corner and joined several other parked cars huddled up against the back of the building.

"But why—" Jason began when his mother had switched off the engine.

"Sorry, no questions now. We're late already."

She led him to an unmarked door, pulled out a key, and opened it. The hallway beyond was dark and empty. Taking a flashlight from her purse, she confidently traced a route through large, echoing rooms and down trash-littered stairs. Finally, at another unmarked door, she knocked. Twice, three times, then once.

"The secret knock is silly," she whispered conspiratorially, "but it appeals to Beardsley's sense of the dramatic."

The door opened and a young, Hispanic-looking man

let them into a fairly large windowless room, lit by a single hanging bulb. In the center stood a battered wooden table and a collection of unmatched chairs. The dozen or so people sitting on them were equally unmatched: men and women seemingly of all ages and social groups.

The large, broad-shouldered man at the head of the table pointed to a couple of empty chairs. "About time, Marilyn. And you know our rule against bringing in new members without approval."

"George Beardsley, don't be pompous. You know very well this is my son, Jason. It's way past time he was brought in on this."

"Perhaps, but—"

"No buts! If you want me here, you take my son too."

Jason felt uncomfortable and confused. But a strange new feeling was growing in him too—pride, pride in his mother.

Beardsley laughed awkwardly and leaned back in his chair. "Blackmail, huh? Well, it was just a formality anyway. Welcome aboard, Jason."

Jason mumbled his thanks and sat down, trying to shuffle his seat a few more inches back into the shadows.

"Now, Marilyn," Beardsley continued, "we'd just come to your part of the agenda. Anything to report?"

Mrs. Sikes smiled confidently. "Yes. I've decided to scrap the others I was working on and concentrate on Rogav Jy, the Fleet Commander."

A thin, bald-headed man whistled. "That's aiming pretty high. Isn't he the top dog?"

"That's right, Professor Ackerman. But the more I think about this scheme, the more I'm convinced that's the only way to go. The Tsorians are ruthless, but they're also very leader-oriented. If an abduction is going to do us any good, it'll have to be someone important enough to make them willing to bargain."

Jason tried to look cool and attentive, but it was hard to hide his rising happiness. Just a few hours ago, his life seemed to be falling apart. Now it was all put back together—in an incredible way.

The bald professor was still voicing doubts. "Well, I don't know. I don't know about this whole thing, really. Remember that group in Switzerland who kidnapped some Tsorian administrator? The Tsorians just sacrificed their man and wiped out a good chunk of Lucerne in response."

"That's right," a white-haired lady said, nodding. "I've had no problem with most of our other projects. Circulating pamphlets, or a little sabotage now and then, or that petition drive in the universities to protest exclusion from Tsorian technology. But this seems awfully risky. We don't want our neighborhoods to go the way of the one in Walnut Creek, and they hadn't even kidnapped anybody."

"Yes, I know," Marilyn continued. "But conditions are special now. At the moment, the most important thing to the Tsorians seems to be defeating an attack from an enemy called the Hykzoi. This Rogav Jy has the reputation for being something of a military wonder-worker, and apparently they'll need that since they don't have a particularly large force here. If we snatch him away now, they're likely to forget about saving face and do some serious bargaining to get him back."

"It's a gamble," someone said.

"Sure it's a gamble," responded a man with a short brown beard, pushing back his chair and standing up. A considerable paunch sagged over his belt. "And I don't mind that. But if you ask me, we're dealing with the wrong players. If these Hykzoi are so strong, it's them we should be dealing with. Sure, the Tsorians might throw us a bone or two to get their chief back. But I bet those Hykzoi would give us a lot more. If we could help turn this war in their favor, they ought to be plenty grateful. We could probably call the shots around here."

Jason glanced at his mother. She looked as if she'd just bitten into something nasty. "Jerry, that is a really bad idea. As I understand it, these Hykzoi are not good guys. For all we know, they'd as soon eat us as bargain with us."

"Tsorian propaganda," the other jeered. "You've been working with those purple monsters too long. You're going soft on them."

Jason tensed, and beside him his mother seemed to bristle like a cat. "Jerry Barns, you have no right to say that. I have more reason than most to hate the Tsorians, and you know it."

"Sure, sure, don't get riled. But you've also worked with them enough to get a little brainwashed. Why should we trust everything you say about them now?"

Several voices were quickly raised in objection, but to his own surprise, Jason's was the loudest. "Because she's the one you've had do your dirty work all these years. She's the one who's had to put up with those creatures, so you'd better listen to what she has to say about them!"

Jason looked down and blushed, not so much from his brashness as from the fact that a few hours earlier he'd harbored even worse doubts about his mother. He smiled awkwardly when she reached over and squeezed his hand.

"Let's try to keep down the name-calling," Beardsley said severely. "What do the rest of you think of Jerry's idea?"

Professor Ackerman cleared his throat. "It's interesting

but hardly workable. We've no reason to believe these Hykzoi would be either better or worse than the Tsorians. And you know the old saying about the devil you know."

"Besides," said the young man who'd opened the door, "how do we even contact them? Or what language do we use? At least the Tsorians have learned English."

Seeing the nods of agreement around the table, Beardsley said, "All right, let's table Jerry's approach for a while and decide what ransom we'll ask from the Tsorians. It's got to be something worth the risk."

Jason sat quietly as discussion swirled around him. Professor Ackerman, an astronomer, wanted to force the Tsorians to share their achievements in space science and medicine and all the other advances that frustrated humans felt extraterrestrial contact should have brought them. Others were for demanding Tsorian withdrawal at least to their Mars base, while the majority, led loudly by Jerry Barns, wanted complete Tsorian withdrawal from Earth's solar system. After a time, Jason tuned it out. His brain was already on overload. It was enough to bask in the fact that he was a Resister and the son of Resisters.

At last the meeting broke up, and by ones and twos the conspirators slipped out to their cars. Jason welcomed the cold, ocean-scented slap of fog. It seemed to set a seal of reality on the evening.

As they left the parking lot for the bleak, foggy streets, his mother said, "Thanks for coming to my aid in there. Most of the others are okay, but that Jerry Barns is an unmitigated jerk."

"Yeah, he sure is." Jason blushed and looked out the window. "I . . . I guess I have been too, Mom. I'm sorry."

She smiled at him, then looked back at the road. "That's all right, kid. I'm sorry too. I shouldn't have kept you in the dark, but somehow after what happened to your dad . . . And then there was the Walnut Creek group. I knew Ricky Jensen's parents. They were so proud of their son. I'm proud of mine too and just didn't want to risk losing him."

"Hey, Mom. Nobody's going to lose. Except the Tsorians. With us working together, they're doomed."

Their laughter filled the car, and for the moment, Jason felt every bit as confident as his words.

✦ f i v e ✦

JASON TRIED NOT TO CRINGE AS THE GIRL'S CLAWS SCRAPED across his palm. His mother had said that Tsorian use of the human handshaking custom showed respect, but somehow the girl's expression did not seem very respectful. It looked more like she'd just touched something slimy from under a rock.

Then a diplomatic, sharp-toothed smile slid over her face. Not to be outdone, Jason smiled back, trying desperately to think of light conversation. There was something he'd noticed in the introductions the Fleet Commander had given.

"Eh . . . when your father introduced you just now, he called you his bond-daughter. What does that mean?"

Jason thought he saw a flicker of exasperation on Aryl's face as she glanced to where her father was seated with Jason's mother in a nearby part of the Headquarters lounge. Quickly she looked back and said in her oddly accented English, "You really know nothing about that?"

"No, nothing."

With a suppressed sigh she gestured to a couple of free-form chairs and took a seat. "We Tsorians spend the first years of our lives on nursery planets growing up with

34

others our age, learning a little of everything—arts, music, history, philosophy, and all the sciences, of course."

"You don't live with your parents?" Jason asked, surprised.

"Of course not. The only adults there are the instructors and such. Naturally we know who our parents are. We keep very close watch on their careers, and occasionally one or both might come by for an acquaintance visit."

"Sounds pretty grim."

Briefly, she looked annoyed. "No, not at all. It is very pleasant. There are no rank distinctions then, so you can associate with whomever you want. And you can play. There are few responsibilities except to learn. But then comes the First Passage, and all that changes."

Despite himself, Jason was getting interested. "So what's that?"

"It comes at what must be about your age of twelve. It's then that a child must choose which parent to bond to. The child then becomes an adjunct to that person, joining him or her and taking on the same rank and career track. All learning from then on is what the parent sets out as being essential to that career."

"So you chose your father to be bonded to because you wanted to be a Fleet Commander?"

The stare from her black hamster-eyes made him feel squirmy.

"By the time of my First Passage, my mother had died. She was a strike squadron commander and was killed in a skirmish with the Skreel. But I probably would have chosen my father anyway. He is something quite special. He demands a lot, but I am learning a lot too. Our bonding is very strong."

She flicked a claw against a piece of floating sculpture.

With a jangle all the pieces bobbed and spun, rearranging themselves in a new pattern. The metallic noise grated against the quiet Tsorian music that always thrummed through the lounge. Some background music, Jason thought. The throbbing gurgles sounded more like backed-up drains.

Nervously Jason glanced to where his mother was chatting with Commander Rogav about this war they were having with the Hykzoi. He marveled at her cool. He himself felt as tight as a spring and about as subtle as an elephant. Surely it must be stamped all over him that he was here as a Resister kidnapper and not because he wanted to dine with these creeps.

Guiltily he looked back at the girl. She seemed tense but not suspicious. Not that he was sure he could recognize either in a Tsorian. He'd better keep her talking. She was looking at him with an expression that seemed straightforward enough—arrogant annoyance.

"You . . . eh, you mentioned a 'First Passage.' Is there some sort of 'Second Passage' too?"

"Of course! You certainly are . . . unfamiliar with Tsorian ways, aren't you? The Second Passage comes at the end of the bonding period. There's a sort of evaluation of your aptitudes and skills. Then you pass into adulthood with a rank and career track of your own. Often it is similar to that of your bond parent."

"So you'll become a fleet commander?" Jason was genuinely surprised. What a system. For the first time he heard a Tsorian laugh, a dry, crackly sound.

"Hardly! Well, it's possible, of course, were I to pass into command rank, but there are many different stages in any rank. My mother was much lower in the scale of command, but she still shared my father's rank so it was permissible for them to have social contact."

"You mean . . . ?"

Aryl glanced quickly to where her father had just stood up. She seemed relieved. "It's time for us to go up and dine."

Rogav lead the party to a bank of lift tubes, stepped into one black opening, and disappeared. Marilyn gave Jason a brief encouraging smile and followed suit. Jason looked at Aryl. Her smile was unmistakably smug. With exaggerated ease she stepped into another black opening and vanished, leaving Jason suddenly alone.

He swallowed down panic and stared at the opening before him. It wasn't just a hole, it was a featureless void. But he'd have to step into it; he couldn't let his mother go into this alone. Fighting not to close his eyes, he stepped forward.

Black nothingness engulfed him. He was standing on nothing solid, yet somehow something was holding him and even moving him upward.

After a moment the blackness in front of him shimmered, and as if through a veil, he could see a lighted scene with the others waiting for him. Gratefully he leaped out.

Again his mother's quick smile was mocked by the smugness on the alien girl's face. We ought to kidnap her while we're at it, he thought, not that anyone would want her back.

Fighting the last of his queasiness, he followed the others. Clearly they were now much higher up in the conical Headquarters tower because the transparent outer walls had a more noticeable curve. They entered an area where irregularly shaped tables seemed to rise out of the floor like mushrooms. The Tsorians, clustered on the floor around some of them, hastily gave their commander an open-clawed salute. Absently Rogav acknowledged these as he led his group to a small table abutting the transparent wall and sat on the lushly carpeted floor.

Jason couldn't help but be impressed with the view.

It was spectacular. Though still far from the top of the tower, they were higher than any human skyscraper. To the south, San Francisco glowed with light, and to the east the velvety dark hills seemed strewn with jewels. Between them, the blackness of the bay was spanned by four slender bridges that glimmered like dew-hung spiderwebs.

When Jason finally forced his attention from the view, he realized Rogav was speaking.

"Your ancestors evolved from less carnivorous sorts than ours, but our nutritional requirements are not unlike. I hope the same can be said about our ideas of 'tastiness.'"

He pulled a short, square column out of the table's center, jabbed at some controls, and within moments a patch of blackness appeared in its side. Rogav reached in and withdrew four platters and four high-sided bowls. Drinking-cups, Jason decided as he eyed the bluish liquid sloshing in his. The contents of the platters were even more questionable.

Rogav apparently noticed his and his mother's doubtful expressions. "Vegetable matter crisped around meat—some is even locally grown." Picking up a long tubular scoop, he jabbed into his own plate with the two prongs at the scoop's end.

Jason looked across the table at the plate in front of Aryl. It was full of quivery gelatinous stuff, sort of like gray tapioca. Suspended in it were round, purplish things that she was jabbing at and popping into her mouth. Jason felt ill.

His own meal, a heap of little greenish curls, looked uncomfortably like insect larvae. Gingerly he prodded one with his prong, then hurriedly stuck it into his mouth. It crunched. Please be vegetables and meat, he thought, forcing himself to swallow and poke at another one.

As he chewed, he glanced up at Aryl. There she was again, radiating smugness, probably expecting him to be sick. Well, he wouldn't be. He tried to think of something suave to say. Finally he leaned back and said airily, "Not bad. Have you had much opportunity to taste our food?"

She looked a little surprised. "No, not much. I haven't been here that long."

"Oh, really?" Casually he waved his eating prong toward the view. "And what do you think of this planet of ours?"

She was silent a moment, then answered, "It is interesting, if a little wild. But one thing I don't understand is how you can bear cohabiting with so many subintelligent life-forms."

"Huh?"

"I mean, you hardly modify your environment at all. Plants growing everywhere, and you sort of fitting yourselves around them. Even in the cities there are almost as many plants as buildings. People even have them *inside* the buildings. And little animals too, all sorts of little animals. Quite primitive really."

Right, Jason thought, we like city parks and pet poodles, so we're primitive. Might as well shock her for all it's worth.

"Well, that's the way we like it, and there's not enough of it if you ask me. My mom and I have pet goldfish; I'm trying to talk her into a dog, and we've scads of houseplants. In fact, right near our house there's a park, a big clump of rocks and trees that the city builders just left and built around. Anytime I get upset and want to be alone and think, I go there."

"You go to a rock?" Aryl's shocked expression delighted Jason, but before he could enjoy it fully, an exclamation from Rogav interrupted.

"Ah! There is one of your planet's greatest glories."

"The moon?" Marilyn said. "Don't you have moons?"

"Some planets do, but few that large. The Emperor's own world, Elak Tsor, has only a ring of dust and asteroids. It makes a very pretty glittering, but is nowhere near as grand."

"Well," Marilyn said evenly, "it is comforting to know that there are some things about us you people admire."

"There are many things we admire," Rogav responded. "I've been learning about your past, about your culture. There's much you can offer our Empire."

"But that's what I've been saying. That's the very sort of thing those Resisters so much resent. They wonder what good it is having you admire our past if you take away our future?"

Jason stiffened. His mother was skating on awfully thin ice here. What was she aiming at?

But Rogav seemed to be enjoying the debate. "We haven't taken away your future, we've offered you a new one. Joining the Empire means sharing futures you've never dreamed of."

"I hope you pardon my frankness, but sharing usually means doing things for mutual benefit. A lot of people are wondering where the 'mutual' comes in. I mean, we have been part of your empire for ten years now. Not all humans are Resisters, but a good many do think we ought to get something positive out of this relationship."

Rogav laughed bitterly. "Yes. What is the phrase? 'You've put your claw on it.' If your world had been a normal Imperial acquisition, things would have been different. Much would have opened up for you already. Technology, education, travel throughout the Empire. But as long as your world remains on the edge of Imperial conflict, you'll unfortunately be treated as little more than a military outpost."

"You know what's funny?" Marilyn said, taking a hesitant sip from her drinking bowl. "Before you people showed up, a lot of us imagined that if any alien race survived their own technology long enough to get into space, they wouldn't be militaristic but sort of pacifistic and philosophical."

"Ah, but you see, you were reasoning from the experience and values of your own species." Rogav shook his head. "You may be alarmed by your own militarism, but it is nothing compared to ours. We consolidated our home world into one totalitarian empire long before we had the technology either to blow ourselves up or to get into space. When we did get there, we just expanded the practice. Of course, there are plenty of pacifistic, philosophical species in the galaxy, but naturally they aren't the empire builders, so they weren't likely to be the ones you'd meet first—no more than you'd be likely to meet the least militaristic Tsorians when your first contacts are with the military."

Marilyn nodded thoughtfully. "And then to add insult to injury, after so many centuries of thinking ourselves the most splendid things in the universe, the first aliens we meet simply crack down on our governments and rebellions and otherwise ignore us. I suppose a lot of people feel that if someone had to conquer us, we want them to take us seriously. If they aren't going to obliterate or remold us,

41

at least they could help us. As the phrase goes, 'We want to have our cake and eat it too.' "

"I do take you seriously. But to know if the analogy is correct, I'd need to know what a 'cake' is."

"A cake? Why, that's absolutely basic human cuisine. But you realize, of course, that you're going to have to learn what it is now, because Earth custom demands that if your dinner invitation is accepted, you have to accept one in return."

"A tempting offer, but I'm not sure everyone in this building would approve of the Fleet Commander skipping off to dine in a native home."

"I'm not talking about everyone in this building. I'm talking about you. Besides, I thought you said you took us seriously, quaint customs and all."

"Ah, you have caught me there. I will give it some thought, see how the military situation develops. Now, let me order us another course."

On the drive home, Jason mentally reran the whole incredible evening. Such a contrast to the last time he and his mother had been there together, not so much in what they did, as in his being aware of why they did it. But one thing still made him uneasy.

"Mom," he asked at last, "why did you talk to him so much about what the Resisters think? Wasn't that a little dangerous?"

"I don't think so, Jason. From everything I've heard, this Rogav Jy is a very independent, unconventional sort. I wanted to give the impression that I am too, that I can understand what the Resisters are saying and yet come to my own independent conclusions and act on them. I'm gambling on that being the sort of person he admires—and from whom he might accept a dinner invitation away from Headquarters."

"He didn't actually accept the invitation."

"No, but he didn't refuse it either. And the little challenge I threw in there at the end should help. I get the feeling there are some other authorities at the Headquarters he'd love to defy."

Jason chuckled. "You know, you're getting awfully good at this secret agent stuff. I'm impressed."

"Thanks—I think. But really this whole thing is becoming a lot more difficult than I imagined."

"Hey, no, you're a great Mata Hari, or whoever. You know, that old-time lady spy."

A smile quivered around her lips but quickly vanished. "Thanks, but that's not it. The role-playing is not the hard part. It's that, well . . . the longer I work with the Tsorians, the more I come to see them as—as individuals. Their ideas and actions are wrong, of course, but I can see how they came to them."

"Mom! They're the enemy."

"Jason, I'm not forgetting that. But they're not the *faceless* enemy anymore. That's the problem. It's a lot harder to hate them. And blind hate is what you really need to be good at something like this."

For an unsettling moment, Jason thought he almost understood what she was trying to say. Then he shunted the thought aside. These people were the enemy, pure and simple. They had to be beaten. Any other viewpoint was asking for trouble.

He looked over at his mother. No, they definitely did not need any more trouble.

◈ s i x ◈

WITH THE THREE CLAWS ON HER RIGHT HAND, ARYL loosely gripped the bar. A twist of her wrist, and her whole body rotated slowly around it. Then she let go. The low gravity spin arched her toward a second bar, which she hooked with her knees. She rocked there a moment before swinging around and finally perching on top. Ash-gray hair floated like smoke about her dark face, then slowly settled onto her shoulders.

The low-grav rec facilities here were pretty good, a lot better than on her nursery world, though nowhere near what they were on her father's flagship. Still, it was easier to simply reduce a ship's artificial gravity than negate a planet's real gravity.

Pulling her feet up to the bar, she kicked off toward a complex of hoops and spirals. Jerking suddenly at the trill from the communicator on her belt, she sailed past the bar she was aiming for, flailed at the next, and only caught the last bar by the claws of her feet.

Hanging upside down, she activated the communicator, trying to keep annoyance out of her voice. "Aryl here."

"Rogav here. An Iopheenian Primal is in orbit and has requested a Proximity Conference. This could be important. I would like you to attend. Meet me as soon as possible in environmental chamber number two."

"Yes, sir." Aryl sighed, then let go.

Dropping steadily downward, she grabbed a passing bar for one final spin, then landed gently on the floor and hurried to change out of her exercise suit. A group of several other low-grav enthusiasts were just coming in and saluted her before she'd even fastened her green-lined cape to the shoulders of her black uniform. She acknowledged them, then hurried to the lift tubes.

As Aryl rose toward the proper floor, she forced her thoughts to the subject of Iopheenians. What could be so important about a meeting with one? She'd never paid much attention to them in her studies, beyond their poetry, of course. Iopheenian poetry was drilled into everyone. Some of it wasn't all that bad. There was more to them than poetry, though, but before she'd half sorted it out, she was at the door of the environmental chamber.

Cautiously she walked in, not sure what conditions Iopheenians liked. Apparently slightly low gravity, she realized after a few bouncy steps. And also hot and humid. Running claws through hair that was already becoming lank and damp, she looked for her father. He was seated by a table studying a data screen.

Without looking up, he threw out the expected question. "Aryl, tell me what you know about Iopheenians."

She cleared her throat. "The name comes from a star system in the Grendth sector. The Iopheenians are a very old civilized race. They've inhabited that and several adjacent star systems for . . . for a long time."

"And?"

"They are, eh . . . noted for their devotion to the arts and philosophy, and for their political neutrality."

"The result of which being . . . ?"

"Oh. That they are often called upon to be mediators in interstellar disputes and are given pretty much free right of travel throughout the known galaxy."

"Good. So, the question arises, why should an Iopheenian Primal want to see a Tsorian Fleet Commander? There are no records of any Iopheenian missions in this region, and they generally consider Hykzoi attitudes toward the arts to be irredeemably barbaric, so they're not likely to have much business there. All of which suggests that this Primal may have something to convey to me, though he'll never come out and say it. Iopheenians are maddeningly indirect. Help me listen for it, will you. I wish Subcommander Hlon were here. He could use the diplomatic experience, but he's off inspecting the Mars base. So you'll have to listen twice as hard."

The entry chime sounded, and Aryl looked toward the door. With a mechanical sigh, it opened to its full height to admit the tall diplomat.

On an undulating motion from a profusion of long golden strands, the Iopheenian swept into the room. The curtain of delicate strands cascaded from the uppermost and largest in a chain of golden spheres of diminishing size that made up the body. The lowest, marble-sized segment swung a few feet above the floor. Swaying back and forth between the supporting veil, each ball gleamed with polished brilliance. The second sphere from the top, however, was banded with vibrating purple, which emitted a sound like tinkling chimes.

Having completed the formal greeting, the Iopheenian switched to a language within both species' capabilities. "Fleet Commander Rogav Jy, I am Jargaroovun, Primal Ordinary of the Iopheenian Assembly. I am delighted that fortuitous chance has provided me with the opportunity to visit one of the newest jewels in your resplendent Imperial crown."

"We are honored by your presence, Primal. Anywhere that Tsorians tred is always home to our most valued friends, the Iopheenians."

As the two continued with the diplomatic niceties Aryl's attention wandered from the conversation. So very odd looking, these Iopheenians. Yet despite their extreme alienness they weren't the least repulsive. That was surprising, considering how repulsive she found the natives of this planet. But maybe that was because the people of Earth were not alien looking *enough,* she thought suddenly. Maybe the more a species looks like one's own, the more the little differences stand out. Instead of seeing them as obvious aliens, they look like failed attempts to be like oneself.

The thought made her strangely uncomfortable. She switched her attention back to the conversation, hoping she hadn't missed the hidden message her father was seeking.

"Yes, a Primal sweeps as widely as an Ohmal rage-wind," the Iopheenian was saying. "My journey through this sector to the worlds of the Five Brothers system has been most diverting. It even provided the unexpected pleasure of visiting Ineef. A perfect gem of a world, so splendidly crystalline. My stay there for several of its all-too-brief days allowed me to enjoy its endlessly varied sights. Although I must admit to remorse at owing this pleasure to the woeful state of public health on Umurstis. Another plague, it seems, requiring, of course, the diversion of all interstellar traffic. I heartily trust it is quelled soon, although I myself am selfishly in its debt."

"Ah, an interesting experience, indeed," Rogav said politely. Aryl tried not to fidget as she stood beside him. They could not, of course, sit, as Iopheenian anatomy made it impossible for their guest to do so. "And the rest of your journey was uneventful?" the Commander continued.

"Life is never without event, Commander. The little multipedal folk of Krif III requested an Iopheenian mediator for one of their endless swarm-holding disputes, a simple matter really. Then between there and E'Nti, the ship's propulsion unit developed something called a 'reactive overlap,' a confusing technical matter that thankfully could be left to the technicians."

To obey her father, Aryl was straining to follow all of this, but she couldn't see how any important message could be buried in this travelog. The two moved to a discussion of the new bardic academy on one of the Five Brothers worlds. Then the conversation turned to poetry, and Aryl finally tuned out. She'd read more than enough Iopheenian poetry. There were two schools she remembered: the short, simple works and the long, convoluted, boring ones. She suspected this Iopheenian, were he a poet, would represent the latter.

Finally the conversation moved into concluding formalities, with Aryl still shifting uncomfortably from one foot to another. All the while the Iopheenian had ignored her presence, showing his appreciation of Tsorian custom in treating a bond-child as an extension of the adult. Preferable to dealing with the uncouth local aliens, Aryl thought, since it spared her having to think up innocuous conversation.

At last, the Iopheenian jangled through his farewell dance and swept from the room. As the door contracted behind him, Aryl dropped into a chair. With a laugh, her father did the same.

"Well, Daughter, did you catch it?"

Aryl tensed up. Quiz time. "A message, you mean?"

"Yes, a jewel buried beneath all that garbage. Come, think back. What did he say first?"

Desperately she thought back. She'd tuned out the greeting. But then he'd gone on. "He said something about Primals being like Ohmal rage-winds."

"Ah, very good. You picked that up."

Aryl was startled but tried instead to look sage and thoughtful.

"Yes," he continued happily. "Ohmal rage-winds are notorious for all the flotsam and jetsam they pick up. So right away he was telling me he had picked up some information. And did you catch where he'd hidden it?"

Mentally she rummaged around again. "Well, he talked about all those planets, the quarreling little people with lots of feet, and the pretty crystal world he was able to gush about because a plague on . . . on Umurstis diverted him there."

"That's it, right there! All that talk was in aid of one sentence. The one about how he'd been diverted from Umurstis because of one of their outbreaks of plague."

"Well . . . eh, don't they have plague? I mean, I thought they did, regularly."

"They do! Very regularly. Every twenty-three to twenty-five Imperial years."

Aryl tried not to look as blank as she felt.

"But you see, the last outbreak was only nineteen and a half years ago, so the diversion of shipping, no matter what the authorities said, must really have come from some other cause. And what is there outstanding about Umurstis besides plagues?"

Aryl shook her head. She'd just exhausted her knowledge of Umurstis.

Rogav answered his own question. "Statrozine. Umurstis is one of the major galactic centers for mining statrozine."

Now Aryl brightened. She knew about statrozine. "And statrozine is an essential element in the cooling system of Hykzoi warships."

"Right! And it gets better. The closest Hykzoi base to Umurstis where statrozine can be refined is Binitrivi, and Binitrivi is right in the heart of the Qvi-Nars Corridor."

"And that is right in the center of the Hykzoi area where our probes have been reporting unusual activity!"

"Exactly!" Rogav laughed triumphantly.

Aryl felt as exhausted as if she'd run a race. But her father took no breather before turning his conclusions into actions. He jabbed at his communication console.

"Theelk, contact Subcommander Hlon on Mars. He is to immediately take charge of the Fleet vanguard, while they commence preparations for departure to the Qvi-Nars Corridor." The Commander paused and a slightly malicious smile spread over his craggy face. "And notify Governor Oimog that I am immediately recalling all of our strike ships from occupation duty. She can play petty dictator on her own, now."

Closing communications, Rogav got up and strode to the transparent wall. He saluted toward the landing derrick where the Iopheenian's ship was already preparing for departure. "Thank you, Primal Jargaroovun, for your interesting little monologue. I wish you a continued pleasant trip."

Aryl watched as one tendril of the landing derrick slowly uncoiled upward and released the opalescent egg that was the Iopheenian ship. It hung suspended for a moment then swiftly rose into the alien blue sky.

Aryl turned and smiled at her father. "Does this mean we'll be leaving here and going into action soon?"

"Yes, and about time too." He gestured to the rumpled hills, now golden in the light from the planet's westering sun. "Not that this world is all that bad, as primitive outposts go. An interesting people too, full of potential— at least they would be if small-minded political appointees like Oimog could keep their claws off them.

"But Aryl, you and I aren't bureaucrats, or even diplomats. We're soldiers. We don't belong on this or any planet. We belong out there." His gesture seemed to tear at the air and light that hid them from the stars.

Commander Rogav walked back to his desk and threw himself comfortably into a chair. "But things won't be ready for a while yet. We still have a bit of waiting in store." He turned thoughtfully toward his communications console. "Maybe the time has come to take that native woman up on her invitation."

Aryl shrugged and turned back to look at the alien landscape, realizing suddenly that every landscape she'd see for the rest of her life would probably be as alien. She tried not to hear her father's conversation with the native employee.

But still, she couldn't really approve. Understand maybe. Eve of battle and all. And even if more choices were open to someone of her father's rank, he'd still probably be attracted to the unconventional.

Still, these creatures were so . . . alien. She shrugged again. Well, at least this invitation, in native fashion, seemed to have been confined to the adults. She doubted if she could take another moment with that native boy. For days she'd felt guilty because she'd not been quite as diplomatic as she might have been with him. But all that really didn't matter now.

A smile crept over her face. In a short while, nothing about this world would matter. They'd be out where they belonged, among a whole new arrangement of stars.

seven

JASON FORCED HIMSELF NOT TO HURRY. BE COOL, HE TOLD himself, slow and casual, just like walking home from school on any normal day. Deliberately he looked at each house and garden as he sauntered past. And suddenly it struck him. He might not see any of them again.

Year after year, walking home from one school or another, he'd passed these houses or ones like them. And tomorrow he might be dead. At the very least, he'd be different. He'd be part of a major revolutionary action, or a major crime, depending on the point of view. In any case, he'd not be the same little kid who'd trudged unnoticingly past these gates and flower beds, mind on homework or on who was bullying whom at school. The thought excited—and frightened—him. It was like standing on the high-diving board, poised to leap.

Before he realized it, his own house was before him. Quite a nice place really, in a modest, pseudo-Spanish sort of way. The roof was red tile, the walls rough stucco, and the doors and windows were arched. In a niche by the heavy wooden door, St. Francis stood, benignly feeding birds. A wry smile crept across Jason's face. A very human saint this. A Tsorian saint would never feed birds.

Businesslike again, he walked up the ivy-bordered path and let himself in with his key. He glanced at the grandfather clock ticking ponderously in the hall. Two hours before his mother and her guest were due. Plenty of time to get ready.

First he went around the house, watering plants and filling the automatic feeders on the fish tanks. His packing had already been done. For days he'd been slipping a few of his things over to the Morganthalls' house every time he went to water their plants. The neighbors wouldn't have noticed since he'd been plant-sitting there for months while the Morganthalls were in Europe. All he had to do now was get his station here ready, and wait.

Unhooking the little slatted doors, he let them swing shut in front of the breakfast nook. Like miniature saloon doors, they cut off the built-in table and its wraparound bench from the rest of the kitchen. Then he set about gathering quilts and making a nest for himself at the back of the horseshoe where he could peer out the kitchen window through the half-open slats of the venetian blinds.

Jason looked out now. His deliberate calm squeezed away. They were out there, his fellow conspirators, already in place and waiting. Up until now it had just been a plan, almost a game. But now people besides himself were acting on those plans. It was almost five P.M. Carlos Alvarez was parked across the street, and Jerry Barns and several others would be parked farther up. At a signal from him . . .

Signal! Jason jumped up, ran into his bedroom, and grabbed the flashlight. He checked the batteries. Good. Heading back through the kitchen he stopped for a moment and eyed the chocolate cake his mother had baked for that night. Regretfully he turned aside and grabbed some cookies and a couple of apples instead. The oven timer had turned on, and the smell of pot roast was already tantalizing.

Settling into his nest, Jason arranged himself so that if someone of Tsorian height should casually look over the swinging doors, he'd be hidden by the overhang of the table. If he were seen, well, then he'd say that he'd meant to leave for a friend's house earlier but had fallen asleep doing homework. He had an algebra book there as a prop, but was much too tense to even think of equations.

Instead he rehearsed their plans again and again, imagining what he'd do in every possible contingency. He was so absorbed in this that the sudden click of the front-door key sounded like a gunshot. Fear and excitement exploded through him, and he scrunched down into the quilt, straining to hear over the hammering blood in his ears.

"Well, this is it," he heard his mother say in the other room. "A reasonably typical human home. Must look pretty primitive to you."

To Jason, the harsh Tsorian accent seemed jarringly alien here. "Not primitive necessarily, but certainly different."

"Yes. Well, have a seat, won't you? That couch is fairly comfortable. What are your houses like, then? Built along the same lines as your Headquarters?"

"Somewhat. We like open spaces, few angles and confining walls."

"Then this place must feel like a cave to you."

The Tsorian commander laughed. "Ah, but your ancestors used to live in caves, didn't they? Ours preferred plains and open hilltops."

"Hmm. Then I'm surprised you didn't set up your main headquarters in Kansas or someplace like that."

"Yes, but we're incorrigibly fond of oceans as well."

There was silence, then a slight tinkling of glass. "What would you like to drink, Commander Rogav? We don't have any of that blue stuff you served, I'm afraid."

"Quite all right. That was a synthesized batch. Not very good. I'll have some of what you call brandy, if you have any. I've enjoyed that before."

Jason tuned out the small talk about drinks. The conspirators had thought about trying to drug Rogav's drink, but they didn't know enough about Tsorian physiology. They couldn't risk poisoning him. So they'd fallen back on this other plan. Just wait until he seemed relaxed and unsuspecting enough, then burst in and grab him.

But Jason didn't like it. He was supposed to wait at least until the two had started eating, but he didn't like *that* at all. He didn't like their using his mother as bait. He didn't like being the one to decide when to spring the trap. They ought to have drugged the drink.

In the front room, the conversation had drifted back to homes. "They can tell you so much about the species that inhabit them," Rogav was saying. "On Aerulj, family is everything, and their homes are just a cluster of clay pods that expand with the family. Or look at this place. There are plants everywhere, sitting on furniture and shelves, hanging from the ceiling. And most of that wall is given over to fish. It wouldn't occur to a Tsorian to share his home with such things."

"From which you conclude we are a pack of barbarian savages."

"Not at all." Rogav paused. "Well, actually, some probably would conclude that. But it's just that your species is among those with a more unitary view of life, tending to view yourselves as part of a whole. Oh, I know your writings say you don't do enough of that, but the fact that this bothers you shows that it is a real value for you. Tsorians in general are more compartmentalized, more structured and goal oriented. Even arts and philosophy are very orderly. It all makes for efficient empire building, but we do miss some of the riches which Imperial contacts could offer."

Jason could hear his mother's voice soften. She should have gone into acting. She was very convincing. "Obviously you're not like that yourself, Rogav, or you wouldn't be sitting here making that observation."

Again a gruff Tsorian laugh. "True. But like you, we are diverse. Generalities stretch a lot."

"So, I'll bet you have a secret room in your home full of hanging plants and goldfish."

"Not likely!" His chuckle trailed off. "Actually, I don't have a home, except maybe my cabin aboard the Fleet's flagship. Many Tsorians do adopt a homeworld, of course, after leaving their nursery planet, but not the military."

"Umm. I suppose military life is about the same anywhere. A girl in every port and so forth."

Instantly, Jason wished his mother had not said that. The Tsorian seemed amused.

"In most of the ports I've been to, you can't even recognize which are the females—if they have them at all."

"Well, at least you military Tsorians have each other. Your ratio of men and women seems about equal."

"True, but that doesn't make much difference when you're at the rank I am. I might as well be isolated on a planet of my own, for all the social contact I'm permitted—with other Tsorians."

Jason did not like the direction this conversation was taking. Apparently neither did his mother. She excused herself to go check on how dinner was doing in the kitchen. Jason half expected her to nod over the breakfast nook door that he should signal the others. But she only clattered about with things in the refrigerator for a moment, then returned to the front room.

This was definitely a dumb plan, Jason decided. There must have been some other way to lure this guy into a trap. What did they know about Tsorians anyway? What exactly would this fast-talking Fleet Commander expect from a "date" with a native female? What would he think she expected?

Jason was half tempted to signal the others now. Instead he sat up and listened tensely to the renewed conversation.

"You know, Marilyn, our species are really quite similar in more ways than general physiology." Jason bristled at that presumptuous alien using his mother's first name.

"Oh, are we?"

"Yes. There's something of a shared spirit. I can see why as a whole you don't take kindly to being conquered. We wouldn't. And yet you have individuals who even though they may not like a situation are willing to work within it and make things better."

"Are you describing yourself, Rogav?"

"Perhaps, but I was intending to describe you. That must be why I find myself so attracted to you, Marilyn. We're the same type of people, despite the unimportant differences."

The answer was too soft for Jason to catch. He strained to hear what was going on in the near silence, all the while blushing at having to do so. This was awful! He was deliberately eavesdropping on his mother and a date on the couch. But the thought of what might be happening in there was worse. He couldn't bear thinking of that alien even touching his mother. Plan or no plan . . .

Jason grabbed the flashlight from the table and desperately began flashing the beam on and off through the venetian blinds. In a moment he saw an answering flash, and several dark figures flitted across the dusk-dimmed street. Jason held his breath, not wanting to hear or think. Suddenly the silence in the next room was broken by the crash of the front door bursting open.

"All right, Tsorian," Jerry's voice boomed. "Get your filthy claws off that woman or I'll slaughter you right now!"

A rustling silence. "That's better. Now, put all the little gadgets on your belt down on that table—carefully—no tricks. I don't want to ruin Marilyn's lovely carpet by splattering your miserable purple blood all over it."

By now Jason was at the kitchen door taking in the scene. Incongruously it reminded him of a second-rate gangster show. Jerry Barns, standing bearded and belligerent in the open doorway, was certainly playing up to the part. His big, ugly pistol was aimed squarely at Rogav. On one side stood Carlos Alvarez and on the other a fellow named Bill. The latter cautiously moved to gather up the items Rogav had just placed on the coffee table.

Jason looked at his mother as she walked to the far wall, self-consciously straightening her hair. She glanced briefly at Jason, then looked away, her expression tense and unhappy.

If that monster's hurt her, Jason thought, just forget about the ransom, I'll beat him to a pulp.

Carlos stepped in swiftly and tied Rogav's hands behind his back, while Jerry gave Jason's mother a mock salute.

"Good job, Marilyn. Above and beyond the call of duty. We'll take him off your hands now."

Jason was confused by the look of anger she shot Jerry in return. Well, she had a right to be angry, having been put through that. Then he saw the Tsorian's expression as he looked at Marilyn. A look of naked pain and shock.

In moments, Rogav's face hardened and he turned to address Jerry. "You are putting yourself and others in great jeopardy with this action. I advise you to cease it immediately."

"Well, I suppose you do. But let me tell you, buddy, the only one who's in jeopardy around here is *you*. There's a van parked outside. You're going to walk with us and get into the back of the van. And do it quietly. Your stinking purple blood wouldn't look any better on Marilyn's flower beds than it would on her rug."

His mother brushed past Jason as she hurried through the kitchen door. There'd been tears on her face. Worried, he returned to the kitchen and walked to where she was leaning against the sink.

"Mother, are you all right?"

"Yes, it's just that I didn't know that it would hurt so much."

"Did he hurt—"

"No! Not him. It's what *I* did. What I had to do. I just didn't realize . . . Never mind. We're in this too deep now to look back. You go with the others in the van. I'll drive our car and meet you at the warehouse." Without even grabbing a coat, she hurried out the back door.

Frowning, Jason returned to the other room in time to see the three men bustling their captive out the front door. The big gun was pressed into the folds of the Tsorian's green-lined cape. In the streetlight glow, Jason could make out a gray van with someone seated behind the wheel.

He closed the door behind him and, with a sudden sense of finality, locked it. Don't even try to think about the future, he told himself as he hurried down the flagstone path. The present was more than enough.

Jason reached the van just as Jerry shoved their prisoner inside. Rogav landed heavily on his side, but despite having his arms bound behind him, he quickly rolled over and sat up.

"Don't try any fancy escapes," Jerry warned him. "Despite what I said in there, I'd love an excuse to kill you."

Jerry and Carlos climbed into the van, gesturing for Jason to join them. Bill slammed the door shut and went to join the other person in the cab. Moments later they were rumbling down the street, the three humans seated near the door on the jolting floor of the van, the Tsorian crouched against the metal wall at the front. Jason could read only cold disdain in his expression now.

"You realize, of course," Rogav said, "that this is an extremely foolish act; the retaliation will be horrendous. But it is still not too late. If you release me, retribution can be kept to the minimum."

"Shut up, Tsorian," Jerry growled. "You're not in charge here. We are."

"There is no way you can benefit from this."

"Don't give us that, freak! We know all about you and what you're supposedly worth. Inside information, remember?" The look that flashed across Rogav's face made Jason wish he were somewhere else.

After long minutes of tense silence, the van came to a halt and the back door was flung open. Jason gratefully stepped out into the cold. The parking lot was just beginning to lose itself in fog. Behind the warehouse there were a far greater number of cars than he'd seen there before.

He followed the others as they hustled their captive through the back door and down the maze of bleak corridors and stairways to the same windowless room he had been in before. The chairs and table had been pushed back, and the room was crowded with people, most of whom Jason had never seen. His mother stood a little apart from the rest, looking pale and strained.

The muttered conversation in the room died as Rogav was led in. Jason perked up a little at the looks of admiration that the crowd gave them all—the daring group that had pulled off the capture.

Beardsley beamed. "Well, the conquering heroes return. And with the prize properly bound and humbled, I see."

The look Rogav raked them with seemed anything but humble. "This action is a very serious mistake on your part. You will reap nothing but extensive retaliation for it."

"We have reason to believe otherwise, Tsorian," Beardsley said confidently. "They won't risk retaliating and forcing us to kill you, because of your stupid little space wars. They'll want you back, and we intend to squeeze all that we can out of it."

"What happens if they don't want him back?" someone from the crowd asked.

"Then we'll have the great pleasure of killing him. But it is on the assumption that this will not happen that you're all here this evening. You've all lost a lot and risked a lot with the Resistance over the years. And not all of the people you've been fighting for have appreciated you nearly enough. The least you deserve is a chance to see one of these beasts at our mercy for once."

Rogav's icy glare swept over the crowd again, stopped briefly at one figure, then moved on. "I'm afraid your understanding of our people is somewhat incomplete. True, as an individual, I am of some value to the Empire. But Tsorian policy never places the worth of one individual above the needs of the whole."

A short, stocky man stepped out of the crowd, his face contorted with barely suppressed rage. "That's right. Individuals never have counted for much with you people, have they? Like when you made an example of Resisters in San Jose by wiping out whole city blocks. My wife and daughter were shopping there. Just a couple of the unimportant individuals you dealt with."

Rogav looked at the man. "True, many of those deaths were regrettable—"

"Regrettable? Oh, I'll give you regrettable!" In one move the man lunged forward and brought an empty bottle down on the side of Rogav's face. The Tsorian staggered, and with a groan he sank to his knees.

In the stunned silence, the only sound was the dripping of blood, alien purple blood, onto the concrete floor.

Suddenly, with animal growls, several others crowded forward and began kicking and hitting their fallen enemy. Years of pent-up hatred were released. At last, one of their omnipotent conquerors would bleed and suffer.

The room erupted in pandemonium. Everyone yelling and shouting and jostling forward, some trying to join the attackers, others trying to stop them. Jason glimpsed his mother forcing her way through.

"No!" she cried. "You can't! We need him!" She and Professor Ackerman threw themselves in front of the attackers, trying to ward off the blows.

Jason wanted to kick and smash as well. But his mother

was there, and probably right, trying to save the creep. He had to help.

Jason jumped in, pulling people away, yelling for them to stop. Eventually the frenzy died into awkward silence. The only sounds were the faint groans from the creature on the floor.

Marilyn was kneeling beside him, his bleeding head in her lap. Jason reached out and clasped her hand, then pulled back. His own hand was now smeared with dark purple blood.

❊ e i g h t ❊

WITHOUT SEEING A THING, ARYL STOOD STARING THROUGH the transparent wall. She was concentrating on remaining calm and in control, as was expected of anyone of command rank. As long as her bond-parent lived, she would continue to share his rank. As long as he lived! She shuddered, then struggled to clamp down on her thoughts. Think only about staying calm.

She felt a touch on her shoulder and spun around to see First Adjutant Theelk smiling wanly at her. Poor Theelk, he was very attached to her father too. They all were. Well, almost all.

Theelk gestured toward the room where they were to meet, a meeting that her rank entitled her to attend. The others gave her encouraging smiles along with their salutes. She could feel it thick in the room. They too wanted her father back.

Quickly the senior Tsorian officers filed in and took up seats around the central desk, Governor Oimog Vak's desk. Aryl studied the Governor and noticed that her blank look of importance couldn't quite conceal a glint of triumph. If there was one person in this corner of the universe who hated Rogav Jy and who would like to see him stay a captive, or worse, it was Governor Oimog. And that same person was now chief Tsorian official on the scene.

"As you know," the Governor said, suddenly quelling the room into silence, "it has been two days now since Fleet Commander Rogav Jy was reported missing. Naturally we have all been very active since then, and it is time for another briefing to pool what we have learned. Could we begin with a report from the chief of security?"

The stocky security chief stood up and gruffly cleared his throat. "As you know, Commander Rogav was last seen in the company of a native employee named . . . eh, Marilyn Sikes. The two departed the Headquarters in the native's ground car, and we understand"—the man glanced briefly at Aryl, then away—"that the Commander intended to dine at the native's home. Upon receipt of this information we proceeded immediately to that dwelling. A meal had apparently been prepared in the cooking area but was never served nor eaten. We could confirm, however, that the Fleet Commander had been there and consumed part of a drink."

There were whispers in the crowd, but the security chief raised his voice slightly and continued. "Let me emphasize that there was no indication of any drugs or poison in the drink. The neighbors were questioned, of course, but gave no information other than the fact that an unfamiliar gray van had parked in front of the Sikes residence during the evening."

"These natives are naturally uncooperative," the Governor commented. "I'll see to it that they pay adequately once this matter is settled. Though, of course, we dare not move against that neighborhood until the Commander's location is determined. Now, have we any report from the Intelligence Department?"

The intelligence chief stood, nervously running a claw along the bridge of her nose. "Sir, as you know, our intelligence network among the natives is very rudimentary."

"I am fully aware of your opinions, Glyr, regarding the administration of this occupation and its intelligence gathering. Please confine yourself to the report."

The intelligence officer lowered her eyes. "Yes, Governor. We examined all the information we could on the native employee Marilyn Sikes, but could find no clear indication of any involvement in Resister activities, though reportedly there are several Resister cells operating in the East Bay area. We are following all leads, and I expect another report momentarily."

Oimog dismissed the intelligence chief with a curt nod and turned to another officer. "Anything further on the Resisters' demands?"

An elderly Tsorian rose to his feet. "The demands seem to have been transmitted from a vehicle-based radio to several native radio stations where they were broadcast as news. You are all no doubt aware of them by now. In essence they offer to return the Fleet Commander in exchange for our abandoning occupation of this planet."

"A patently absurd suggestion," Governor Oimog said blandly.

Aryl's claws tightened into a painful fist, but she tried to look cool and impassive. Beside her, she felt Theelk stir uneasily.

"Governor," he asked, "has Imperial Command been informed of the situation?"

"They will be informed through normal reporting channels, but there is no need for any emergency communication. As governor of this Occupied Planet, I am now in command here, and this has become an internal occupation matter and not a military concern."

Aryl felt like breaking all propriety and shrieking her protest. The others in the room shifted uneasily, and finally the Fleet Engineer spoke up.

"Governor, with all respect, I should point out that the abduction of a fleet's commanding officer just prior to an anticipated attack is legitimately a military concern."

Oimog smiled grimly. "If you consult the regulations, Seg, you will see that in this circumstance it is not. I understand your personal concern, of course. We all admire Commander Rogav." She gave Aryl a smile sweet enough to turn her stomach. "But we cannot let the future of this occupation be jeopardized by emotionalism or by the irresponsible actions of a single fleet officer, no matter how respected."

The murmuring protests were cut short by the sudden entry of an aide who walked swiftly to the chief of intelligence and whispered something in her ear. The officer studied an information printout for a moment, then cleared her throat.

"If I may interrupt, it appears that one of our efforts has produced some information."

In the waiting silence, she continued, "We have discovered the location where Commander Rogav was taken, probably shortly after the abduction. A gray van, matching the description of the one in front of the Sikes residence, was found behind a deserted warehouse in the same city. Analysis shows that a Tsorian, probably the Commander, was recently carried in it."

The officer looked briefly at Aryl, then lowered her eyes. "In a basement room in this warehouse, there had clearly been a recent gathering of natives. And an area of the floor was stained with Tsorian blood."

Aryl felt her body squeeze in on itself. Beside her, Theelk briefly touched her arm and said, "And the blood was analyzed?"

"Of course. It was the Commander's. But I hasten to point out that the quantity of blood was not large enough in itself to suggest a fatal wound."

Dizzily Aryl listened to Oimog's reply. "But it does, however, suggest that we would be ill-advised even to consider negotiating with these barbarians. We cannot trust that we would recover the Commander unharmed or even alive were we to accept their demands."

"Wait a moment, though," Fleet Engineer Seg protested. "If we accept the demands and the natives do not live up to their part of the bargain by returning the Commander in a fit condition, then we need not live up to our part either."

The Governor stood up and glared around the room. "Perhaps, out of deference to everyone's sensibilities, I have not made myself clear. We will not bargain with these hoodlums! If Tsorian occupation forces around the galaxy gave in to every whining demand or act of terrorism, we would never have an empire. Maintaining Imperial honor and policy may, at times, be unpopular and even painful, but I intend to see that it is done."

Engineer Seg was on his feet now too. "But the military situation—"

"—is well in hand," Oimog concluded for him. "Subcommander Hlon is already on his way to the Qvi-Nars Corridor with the Fleet vanguard. That is as it should be, following the order of command and proper procedure. And if we have due confidence in the ability of our military, there should be no further questions. Your absurd faith in the abilities of one undisciplined, renegade officer borders on the superstitious. I will not let it undermine the success of my Occupation."

"Then you intend to leave Commander Rogav in the hands of these Resisters?" Theelk blurted out.

"We will continue our efforts to locate and free him, of course. But I have no intention of negotiating with terrorists."

Aryl glanced nervously at Theelk, then steeled herself to speak up. "But Governor Oimog, surely that is the same as condemning my father to death."

The Governor lavished a cloying look of sympathy on Aryl. "We have no guarantee that he is alive even as it is. But rest assured, I will not actually *reject* their offer; I will simply refuse to respond to it. Our silence may force them to lower their demands until eventually they propose something we can accept.

"Now," the Governor continued as she gazed sternly around the room, "we have spent more than enough time on this vexing matter. Let us return to our duties. I will call you again if there are further developments."

Aryl stalked out of the room, trying to ignore even the sympathy of the others. She was so angry, she wasn't sure she could trust herself to speak to anyone. She wasn't even sure who made her the most angry: the fanatic, deceitful natives, or the arrogant, small-minded Governor. They deserved each other. If only her father and the fleet had never come near this place.

The thought of her father blurred her vision, and she was startled at suddenly feeling a hand on her arm.

She turned to see Theelk standing beside her. Tall and slim with slick black hair, he was quite a contrast to her father's confident sturdiness, and as a stickler for propriety he'd seemed perpetually pained by the Commander's unconventionality. Yet he was Rogav's adjutant, and Aryl knew he was deeply devoted to him.

"Don't let Oimog's needling get to you, Aryl. Your father is almost certainly still alive. If he weren't, the Resisters would not be attempting to bargain."

Aryl managed a smile. "Thank you, Theelk. I just can't help feeling that Oimog is enjoying this situation immensely."

"She is, which shows what a petty, vindictive mind she has. It seems that your father made a far more dangerous enemy in her than he realized. And I'm afraid this waiting game of hers could be far more dangerous than *she* realizes. While we're waiting for our silence to unnerve the Resisters, the Hykzoi attack is almost certainly drawing nearer. Which all goes to show the weakness of using political rather than military appointees in situations like this. Oimog's grasp of strategy is bureaucratic. She sees no reason why the next in command can't perform in a perfectly interchangeable way. Of course, Subcommander Hlon is a very well-meaning fellow, but he has nowhere near the military experience or intuition that your father has. And with the forces assigned here being already inadequate . . ."

"I know," Aryl said dejectedly, leaning against the smooth transparent wall. "Not only was my father quite convinced that a Hykzoi attack is coming, he was very worried about the outcome."

"Well, you needn't take that worry on yourself. You have quite enough as it is. And rest assured, Glyr and I will see that Oimog's people really do keep up the search for the Commander. We all need him back."

71

Aryl nodded, dismissed the First Adjutant, then turned to the alien landscape spread below her. Hateful barbarian world. It was not only costing her her father, it might cost the Empire this entire sector of the galaxy. Angrily she flexed her claws. She had a violent urge to be as primitive as they, to grab some native and tear it to shreds.

With a scowl Jason grabbed the TV remote control and jabbed the off button. The smiling sports announcer shimmered into grayness. The evening news had told him about the upcoming primary elections, the death of a famous actor he'd never heard of, financial problems in Italy, and miners caught in a cave-in. Then it had gone on to weather and sports. Absolutely nothing about the Tsorian abduction.

There had been coverage that first day, of course, when the Resisters had contacted the radio stations and all the media had run with the story. Then the Tsorian authorities had cracked down, and there had been no further coverage. The one station that had defied the ban had had its transmitter melted, along with its broadcasting studio and staff.

So here he was, Jason thought bitterly, as much in the dark as anyone else. Well, almost. He did know they were holding the hostage at Uncle Carl's cabin on Lake Tahoe. But a lot of good that did him if he himself was hiding safe and sound in the Morganthalls' house some two hundred miles away. That had been the price his mother had extracted for allowing him to be in on the actual abduction, being kept out of the rest. She was worried about the danger if the Tsorians should track them down. Still, danger or not, that's where the action was, and that's where he ought to be.

72

Of course, the Tsorians had swarmed about his own house a couple of blocks from here right after the abduction. They'd probably even visited his school to ask about him. At least that had surely boosted his prestige there, but he dared not go back and enjoy it. He had to stay in hiding, living off food he'd stockpiled, only venturing out after dark, and then just for a walk down to Indian Rock to get some air.

He hadn't even heard from his mother or the others since they'd patched up their battered captive and a group of five had set off with him for the mountains in a second van.

Then suddenly Jason had been on his own. He'd felt rather like a professional spy, attaching the phony license plate to his mother's car and giving part of it a quick spray-on paint job. But the drive back to the Morganthalls' house had not been as grand as he'd expected. He'd only just gotten his learner's permit and was so nervous about making a mistake and getting hauled in by the police that he'd failed to enjoy the freedom of it all.

Now that had been almost two weeks ago, and since then nothing had happened, not even a telephone call. He was left with reading, watching TV, and rerunning that night over and over again in his mind.

His mother had been awfully upset after the Tsorian was attacked. Rogav had finally regained consciousness though, and they'd managed to stop most of the bleeding, but he seemed to be in a lot of pain, as if he'd had some ribs broken—if Tsorians had ribs. And he coughed a lot.

Before leaving in the other van, his mother had taken Jason aside and tried to give him instructions, but halfway through she'd broken into tears and gone on about how she felt like a louse. Rogav had trusted her and even liked her and she'd betrayed him, and now he was hurt and maybe would die, and she had led him to it like a Judas goat.

Then Jason had really blown up, yelling that it was her people who mattered, not that arrogant alien, and if she went soft over him, she'd be betraying them. She ought to be proud of what she'd done, not whine about it.

Instead of yelling back at him, she just looked as if he'd slapped her or something, then turned and joined the others at the van. She'd driven off without Jason's getting to speak to her again. Two weeks, and he hadn't even been able to say he was sorry.

It hadn't been her fault, all that nonsense she'd babbled. She'd had to shoulder so much of this on her own. All those years working among the Tsorians could drive anyone to a breakdown, even someone as committed as his mom.

No, if there was any fault here, he decided firmly, it was with the Tsorians. They'd been the ones to force themselves on this world, meddle in its affairs, and divide its people against themselves. The sooner they were driven out, the better. And if it took deception, battery, and even killing a Tsorian leader to do it, then all right, he thought defiantly, he was proud to be part of it.

He smashed a fist into the couch as if it were the whole Tsorian race.

❖ n i n e ❖

WITH A SCREAM, THE SEA GULL DOVE AT SOMETHING IN THE water, then swooped up, a glint of silver squirming in its beak. Other birds chased after it, crying raucous demands.

Aryl watched, disgusted, but glad to fill her mind with something besides the anxiety of the last few weeks. She could, of course, go up to her quarters and study, but everything she was studying made her think of her father. She felt as if a part of her had been torn away and would keep on bleeding forever.

She turned from the loathsome birds and watched this world's bland yellow sun rise above the distant hills. Something seemed to move through the glare, and she shifted her gaze to see Theelk hurrying toward her.

"Aryl," he said, saluting as he approached, then running a claw nervously through his lank black hair. "There's news of sorts, but it's not good."

Aryl stiffened, but Theelk hastily added, "No, not about your father. Nothing there, except the Resisters issuing another reduced set of ransom demands. I doubt they'll ever be reduced enough for Oimog. But she called a meeting. It just let out."

"And I wasn't invited," Aryl said flatly.

Uncomfortably, Theelk looked away. "We mentioned this, of course, but in her own mind she's convinced that your father is as good as dead, so she is considering you to be rankless and unbonded."

It was Aryl's turn to look away. That hurt like a double blow. Rankless and unbonded, a sorry fate for any Tsorian. But to have known such a bonding, with such a fine person as Rogav Jy, and then to have lost it . . . But no. That was not so! Not yet. She wouldn't let it be!

Angrily she turned back to Theelk. "And so what did this gloating Governor of ours say at her meeting?"

"She gave us a military update. It's bad. The Hykzoi attack must have been launched at nearly the same time our vanguard was dispatched. Subcommander Hlon and his forces were overwhelmed in the Qvi-Nars Corridor. Apparently the Hykzoi fleet is far more massive than anyone expected—except perhaps your father. Reports are very sketchy, but it seems our remaining vanguard ships are retreating here with a hoard of Hykzoi right after them. The body of the fleet is assembling near the Mars base. All ships attached to our base here are being deployed into orbit to protect our holdings on Earth. And the Governor has ordered all nonessential occupation personnel on this planet evacuated to Mars. At least she can recognize reality when it stares her in the face."

Grimly Aryl glanced at the derricks and could see they were already preparing for a massive launch. "And Oimog won't consider trading for my father even now?"

"She considers reliance on him to be illogical and, at the moment, irrelevant. Even some of his strongest supporters are admitting that it might be too late for even Rogav to make a difference."

Aryl nodded. "Yes, maybe so. But surely it's worth the

try. There's so much to lose. Have . . . have there been any indirect efforts to contact the Resisters?"

Theelk looked down. "There's been talk of it, but you know how we Tsorians are about defying direct orders. It probably wouldn't do any good anyway. The Resisters are as stubborn and narrow-minded as Oimog."

"But they're as much at risk as we are if withholding our Commander loses this battle for us."

"True, but even if we could reach them outside of channels, we could never get them to believe that."

Maybe not, Aryl thought, as she watched the first of their blue triangles uncoiling from the derrick, but someone ought to try.

Theelk excused himself and hurried off about his duties. Aryl was about to do the same when the full impact of what he had said hit her. If it was officially accepted that her father was dead, then she *had* no duties. Eventually she'd be reassigned, shunted off to some rankless career. But for now she was simply useless.

Her shock slid into anger, then slowly hardened into resolution. All right, if the system was rejecting her, she'd just move outside it. Other duties still held her, even beyond her former rank.

Before doubt could slow her down, Aryl hurried to her quarters, snapped a hand-held blaster onto her belt, then headed back to the lift tubes. She rode one to the bottom floor and took the exit for the native parking lot. Striding between parked cars, she ignored the startled native employees arriving for work. The shuttle bus had just pulled in. Aryl stood aside until the native workers had all filed out, then climbed in and asked the surprised driver if he was returning to the nearest native town.

"Yes, eh . . . miss, yes, I am," he stammered. This was

the first Tsorian he'd seen close up and certainly the first he'd had on his bus. "I'll be returning to Sausalito to pick up another batch of employees."

"Good, then I'll ride with you." She shook a strand of pale hair out of her eyes and took a seat halfway back.

Nervously the driver started up the engine and got underway, not daring to ask her for the fare.

Aryl stared out the smudgy window at the scenery jouncing by. She'd been out of Headquarters before, but always with her father and always in a smooth-riding Tsorian ground/air car, nothing like this bone-jarring native bus. And always before they'd gone into the big native town of San Francisco. She wasn't exactly sure where this Sausalito was or how to get from there to where she was going. A venture with this many unknowns certainly wasn't one she would have chosen—if there had really been any choice.

The bus shuddered to a halt, and Aryl's attention snapped back as the driver hurriedly opened the door and said, "This is where you get out, miss." The natives about to board stepped quickly aside as she climbed down. She kept her eyes straight forward but could feel their startled stares. They'd probably noticed her green cape. Should she discard it? Would it make her a target for violence? No, she was obviously armed, with the silvery blaster gleaming prominently at her hip. And somehow the green cape made her feel closer to her father.

People on the sidewalk kept staring at her until she took to staring back at them. Then they hurriedly looked away. Finally she decided just to ignore them and turn attention to her surroundings.

On her right, the sidewalk bordered a bank of rough white stones that sloped steeply down to the waters of the bay. Waves sloshed against the stones and steadily rocked the boats moored to jutting piers. The air smelled strongly of salt and decaying life, the pungent alien odor of this world's seas.

Wrinkling her nose, Aryl looked across the street to where odd angular buildings crowded in beside each other. They were such a variety of colors, styles, and materials, it almost hurt her eyes to look at them. Obviously simplicity was not something these people prized.

She noticed one sign in a particular shop window, and waiting for a break in the ground-car traffic, she dashed across for a better look.

Tsorian Souvenirs, the sign proclaimed. Items Exclusive to Sausalito, Home of the Space People. Incredulous, Aryl studied the little Tsorian figures in plastic and metal and wood; the model Tsorian towers; and all the shirts, banners, plates, and other unidentifiable items adorned with pictures of the same. Cheap, tawdry stuff. These unscrupulous natives were turning her people into a tourist attraction! Exploiting them for financial gain!

Indignation surged through her and nearly brought her fist through the shop window. But at the sight of a little green-caped figure, she thought of her father. What would he say at this outrage? To be honest, he'd probably laugh, and say the natives might as well get *some* benefit out of the Tsorians' presence.

Well, if she worked on it, maybe she could come to see it the same way. Though she couldn't manage the laugh. Instead, she glared at the shopkeeper, staring nervously out of his window, and turned away.

Anyway, she thought, she wasn't here to sightsee. As far as she could figure out from what she knew of the area, she had to get across the bay to the town of Berkeley. Her knowledge of written English was pretty good, thanks to her father's insistence, but she couldn't see any sign mentioning Berkeley. This wasn't for want of signs, though. The place bristled with them, telling her where not to park, how fast to drive, and where she could do everything from eating to having her hair redone. What an odd idea. Aryl shook her head in bewilderment. Obviously she'd have to ask a native. Scanning the crowds, she finally picked out a dark-skinned native who seemed to be wearing some sort of uniform. She hesitated a moment, then strode toward him, deciding she wouldn't get anywhere if she acted as timid as she felt. After all, she was one of this planet's conquerors—even if she'd never been alone on an alien planet in her life.

"Sir, I need to know what transport to take to the town of Berkeley."

The man had watched her approach warily, hand resting nervously on the weapon at his belt. But eyeing her blaster, he quickly slid his hand away, using it to punctuate a complicated description of bus stops, transfers, and long delays. When Aryl complained, he suggested she try something called a taxi and pointed to some passing ones before hurrying away.

Anxiously Aryl watched the traffic and studied the method natives used to attract the services of these vehicles. Awfully primitive, dangerous too. But finally she worked up courage enough to step from the curb as one passed and yell, "Taxi!"

The first two sped by, though she was sure they carried no other passengers, but finally one pulled to the curb and the driver looked at her skeptically.

"Could your taxi take me to the town of Berkeley, driver?"

"It could if you have the fare."

That left her stunned. "But I . . . I haven't got any of your currency."

"Then you haven't got a ride to Berkeley either."

The arrogant fool, Aryl thought. Clearly *he* had no idea of the significance of a green cape. That gave her an idea. "Wait!" she called as he started to pull back into traffic. "Wait. I have no native money, but I can give you a Tsorian souvenir much better than that tawdry stuff in the shops. An authentic Tsorian cape, command rank." She reached up, unfastened it from her shoulders, and swirled it over to him.

"Hmm," the driver said. "Yeah, my son'd like this. 'Be the first kid on your block to have a real space cape.' Hah! Okay, get in."

The vehicle was smelly and uncomfortable, but at least she was on her way. She regretted the loss of her cape, but if this scheme didn't work, it wouldn't matter anyway. A lot wouldn't matter.

She was gambling everything on one scrap of conversation and on the knowledge of these natives her father had drummed into her. But even this brief excursion on her own was showing how inadequate that knowledge was. Still, she did know that among natives there was one important distinction that was almost meaningless to Tsorians. Age.

This Marilyn Sikes person, having been central to the abduction and being probably the native most familiar with Tsorians, was now almost certainly wherever Rogav was being held. But she also had a son. Were they Tsorians, it would automatically be assumed that he would be with his parent. But these natives had a peculiar attitude toward such things. If danger were involved, no matter

81

how important the activity, the parent would try to separate the child from it. So, if Marilyn Sikes were with Rogav, Jason Sikes almost certainly was not.

From that point on, Aryl realized, her deductions were a bit shakier. Natives would probably assume that having him stay with extended family (another important native relationship) would be too obvious. Yet they also seemed to have a particular attachment for geographic location. So while he would certainly not risk going back to his own home (people being primitive did not mean they were stupid), he might still be in the same neighborhood.

The taxi driver looked over his shoulder, interrupting Aryl's thoughts. "We're coming up on Berkeley now. Just where do you want to go?"

Frowning, Aryl tried to recall the maps they'd studied during the briefings about the abduction. "Eh . . . there's a long straight street, fairly steep, I think, that runs east-west. At its foot, it forms a circle. Do you know it?"

"Sounds like Marin."

"Let me off at that circle."

The driver nodded, and before long he had pulled up to a curb. "Hope you have enough spare clothing to get back," he quipped as he drove away.

That remark had probably been rude, but she ignored it. Getting back was the least of her worries. She looked around in bewilderment. Even more plants than in San Francisco. All shapes, all colors, they nearly buried the houses. She tried to concentrate instead on the streets.

A number of streets, each with its name sign, jutted out at odd angles from the circle. From the map, she remembered the pattern better than the unpronounceable names. Finally, she decided on one, and still missing the weight of the cape on her shoulders, Aryl began trudging purposefully along it, trying not to show the tension she felt.

She shouldn't really be in any danger. The policy of massive retaliation, wiping out several surrounding blocks for harming a Tsorian, had discouraged many attacks. And without her cape, the blaster was even more visible on her belt. Still, she found this a very nerve-racking walk.

It was midmorning now, and there were not many natives about; those who saw her simply stared. She couldn't tell if these were stares of hatred or curiosity. She didn't care.

As she passed one flower-bordered garden, what appeared to be a very young female was playing in the grass. It looked up and trilled, "Hi! You're a purple space person, aren't you? I like your hair. It looks like my grandma's. It's funny."

Aryl was trying to think what to reply when an adult female came rushing from the house and whisked the giggling girl away. Frowning, Aryl continued up the street. The color wasn't purple anyway, it was maroon.

Still, that was the first native who hadn't looked as if it feared or hated her. It was probably too young to have learned that yet.

ten

AFTER ANOTHER LONG, BORING DAY IT WAS FINALLY GETting dark. At last it ought to be safe to go out. Jason felt like some sort of skulking vampire, cowering indoors by day and only venturing forth at night.

It had been such wonderful weather too, taunting him from outside the drawn curtains. And soon school would be out, the school he hadn't been to in weeks. His schoolmates, including those supposed Resisters he'd been so anxious to impress, they'd all start enjoying summer just as if some history-shaking event weren't taking place.

And maybe it wasn't. Maybe his fellows hiding out in the mountains would get tired of being ignored and just kill the Tsorian. Then probably someplace or other would get blown up in retaliation, and everything would be back to normal. And he'd have missed out on just about all of it. Some heroic adventure.

Pulling his jacket collar up and his hat way down, Jason slipped out the basement door, quietly locking it behind him. Dusk was fairly deep now; all of the neighborhood kids had been called in from play. Behind the warmly lighted windows, families were having dinner, or kids were doing homework—or more likely watching TV. He could see the cool flickering glow behind several windows. Someone was practicing the piano, Kara Weisner probably. She was getting pretty good. Jason felt like a ghost, slipping by unobserved, watching the world of the living.

Ahead loomed the dark bulk of Indian Rock. A comforting friend, always there to put things into the right scale. Not for the first time, he wished he hadn't mentioned the Rock to that awful alien girl, even if it had been meant to shock her. It was something too fine, too Earthly, for one of them even to hear about. Still, he suspected the Rock was strong enough to withstand even that besmirching.

Tonight Jason made his way to the hidden cave in the back, the hideout where he and Ken and Todd had been Robin Hood's outlaws or powerful wizards brewing up spells to defeat the Lords of Dark.

By the well-remembered route, he threaded his way up to the tent-shaped cave, then settled down among the tumbled rocks in front. Their rough surfaces gave back the last of the day's warmth. Looking over the roofs and backyards of the houses down the slope, he could see the darkening bay and the sky, its edge still holding a last tinge of pink. Doves called into the soft evening air, and traffic rumbled distantly. In the coolness around him hung the tangy smell of laurel and eucalyptus, and a faint trickle of honeysuckle.

Somehow it was easier to think here. But really, he had already made up his mind. If he didn't hear from anyone soon, say two days, he'd get into his mother's car and drive up to Uncle Carl's place. He hadn't done it earlier for fear that the Tsorians might have found him out and been waiting for a chance to follow him.

But he'd seen no indication of anything like that, and he

was getting dreadfully anxious about what was going on in that cabin. He definitely didn't like his mother being shut up with that alien even if there were others there to keep an eye on him. Of course, the Tsorian probably had been too battered to cause much trouble, but his mother had seemed to be getting a little soft on the guy. Not that he was really all that bad for a Tsorian, but . . . No, Tsorians were bad, and that was that. He simply didn't want his mother to have to deal with them anymore.

The only drawback to his plan was that he really wasn't sure about driving the car. He'd only gone out with his mom a few times after getting his learner's permit. He'd been scheduled to take driving classes, but that was out now, of course. Still, it oughtn't to be too tough. Not if he didn't try it on a weekend.

A dry trickling of pebbles behind him. Quickly he looked around. The cave was dark and quiet. No, there was something there, darker than dark. Slowly it was moving down from the upper cave, way in the back. Wild animals! He'd always imagined they lurked here at night. But this was big.

"Jason Sikes," a voice said from the darkness, "is that you?"

The voice was chillingly accented. He stood up. "Who's there?"

A figure stepped out into the dusky light. Fear rippled through him, and he turned to run.

"Don't!" the Tsorian voice commanded, but Jason was already pelting like a goat down the rocky draw.

Suddenly the air flared blue in front of him. When he could see again, the rocks and bushes that had been there were only smoking ash. In shock he turned around. Light from a distant streetlight glinted in Aryl's black eyes and on the silvery weapon in her hand.

"You must not run off. I need to talk with you."

"Just because you thugs have found me, doesn't mean I'll tell you anything or lead you anywhere." Jason was surprised at how little his voice was quavering. "Go ahead, call the others and haul me away if you want. It won't do you any good."

"Stop chattering, and come back up here and sit down. It's I who have to talk to you, and there aren't any others."

"Sure. You came here by yourself for a friendly personal chat." He tried to sound jaunty and defiant, but all the same he walked up and sat down where she pointed. It helped hide the fact that his legs were shaking. There was nothing left of those bushes but blowing ash.

"I've come to tell you that your people must release my father."

"Ho hum."

"Do not make fun! You have no idea, you myopic troublemakers, what a disaster you are causing."

"So, comply with our demands and the disaster is over."

"No, that's what I am trying to tell you, you thickheaded barbarian! *We* cannot comply with those demands. We have no power to."

"Then get the power."

"Idiot! You've jumped into a political situation you don't understand in the least, and now you've made a mess of everything."

"If you mean that Hykzoi thing, we understand that all right. You've got a war on your hands. So if you want your wonder-working general back badly enough, you'll trade for him."

Aryl stomped her booted foot, and irrelevantly Jason

found himself wondering if they had claws on their feet too. "No, fool! I mean internal politics. Factions! In the absence of the Fleet Commander and the Subcommander, the Governor is in charge, and Governor Oimog hates my father. She wouldn't trade a claw-paring for him."

"So what about this big Hykzoi attack, then?"

"Oimog doesn't know the first thing about military strategy. All she understands is keeping her claws on political power. Besides, she doesn't believe my father can make any difference in the war."

"So maybe he can't."

Aryl snorted derisively, then after a moment lowered her voice. "Maybe, maybe not, but we've got to try everything." Agitatedly she paced the narrow floor of the cave. Jason eyed her weapon, judging his chances of grabbing it from her. Not as good as in the movies, he figured. Suddenly she turned on him.

"There's no point in keeping it from you. The Hykzoi have already launched their attack. They've defeated our vanguard and are headed here. Even now they might be engaging the rest of our fleet—right here in this peaceful little solar system of yours. You might be days away from becoming part of the Hykzoi Empire!"

"So big deal! What difference does it make whose slaves we are?"

"Oh! You deserve to find out just what difference it would make!"

Jason was begining to feel a little braver now. He hadn't been hauled away for interrogation yet. No ghastly torture devices. Maybe she was alone after all.

"So now that you have delivered your message and I have stated our reply, may I go?"

"You cannot fool me that easily. You are a child, and

I know enough about your culture to know that you have no authority to accept messages or make decisions. You will take me to where the others are holding my father, and I will speak with them."

Jason tried to look cool, casually stretching his legs. "As you say, I have no authority. So I also have no authority to take you there. They haven't been in contact. I can't even be positive where they are now." Humiliating to admit, but conveniently it was true.

"Can you tell me nothing of their hostage's condition?"

"What do you mean?"

"Don't play dumb! We found that warehouse where you'd taken him, and we also found his blood on the floor. Tell me, is he hurt? Is he . . . is he dead?"

He'd been about to snap back a defiant answer, but her tone on that last question had suddenly changed. The guy was her father, after all. "I don't know that either. I guess he's alive. He was when I saw him last."

"You were there? Was he beaten, tortured?" She gripped her blaster with renewed ferocity.

"Calm down! It wasn't planned. Some people just lost their cool and battered him around some. We didn't want him killed. What good would a dead hostage do us?"

"Ah." She relaxed and looked away a moment. Jason tensed, then struck at her like a snake, grabbing her wrist and smashing it against a rock. The blaster described a high silver arch through the air and disappeared into a tangle of honeysuckle.

Screaming with rage, Aryl raked her free hand across Jason's face, gouging three red clawmarks down his cheek. He yelped, then punched her in the stomach. Doubling up, she suddenly twisted aside, wrenching her other hand free.

For a moment Aryl leaned against the cave wall, panting and glaring at Jason. Then she launched herself at him again, claws extended. Desperately he jumped aside, feeling one claw gouge his shoulder. Spinning angrily around, he aimed a blow at her head. She dodged and hooked a leg behind his, sending him sprawling to the ground. Before he regained his breath, she leaped on him like a lion. Frantically he grabbed her wrists before she could shred him any further.

Over and over they rolled in the dust outside the cave until finally he had her pinned flat on her back. She struggled to get a foot up to kick him. He was doubly glad she wore boots. All he could think about was the way neighborhood cats disemboweled squirrels.

Her black eyes blazed up angrily at him. Suddenly they widened, and her expression moved from hatred into astonishment and fear. It was just a trick, he knew. He tightened his grip.

But she seemed to have forgotten he was there. "Look! They're here. Already. Oh, please no!"

Jason was tempted to look around at the sky too, but he didn't budge. "Cut it out! I'm not that much of a fool."

Her gaze shifted to him again. "Oh, but you are. You've let the Hykzoi in."

A distinct thrumming from overhead finally made him crane back. There were lights in the sky that weren't stars or airplanes.

Violently his captive jabbed a knee in his stomach and twisted free. But she did not run. When the pain subsided, Jason looked up. The Tsorian was standing only a few feet away from him, looking with horror at the sky. He stood shakily and followed her gaze.

✠ e l e v e n ✠

THE NIGHT ABOUT THEM WAS STREAKED WITH LIGHT, RED light. Glowing red objects darted about or hung suspended in the sky like exotic fish in a huge aquarium. Only they were shaped like rings, rings of red light with thick cross-bars across the middle. They were appearing out of the east, a dozen, then more.

"Look!" Jason heard Aryl exclaim. He turned around to see her pointing to the west, across the Bay toward Sausalito. Tiny blue triangles were swarming there like angry bees. "Is there somewhere we can see, away from this wretched vegetation?"

Jason didn't bother to defend his planet's trees. He too wanted to see. "This way!"

He darted along a narrow cleft between two rock walls, scrambled over a boulder, then crawled up one of the more treacherous cliff routes to the top. He didn't know how well Tsorians climbed rocks. If she fell or got lost, tough.

He hadn't been standing a moment on the bare rock summit, however, when Aryl was beside him. If she'd intended a comment on the route, it was obscured by the sudden sizzling from above.

A stretch of night sky seemed to quiver like air over a

91

candle, and one of the distant blue specks flared into orange. Then the whole sky was in turmoil. Rippling waves pulsed back and forth. Blue and red ships wove a frenzied pattern through the sky, while here and there the pattern was torn with flames and the fall of fiery debris into the Bay or the sprawling cities below.

Both Jason and Aryl were soon cowering down on the rock, frightfully exposed yet unable to take their eyes from the sky.

They said nothing, watching as the blue specks became fewer and fewer in number. Suddenly a wall seemed to hit them, a concussion of sound and force that rolled across the Bay like an impossible tidal wave. It flattened them to the rock like fallen leaves. When, among a litter of roof shingles and broken tree branches, they struggled to sit up, a tall column of fire was rising from the darkness north of the Golden Gate. It climbed higher and higher into the night, a colossal pillar of billowing flame.

Aryl's breathing was sharp and ragged. The Tsorian Headquarters. Jason had a crazy urge to put an arm around her shoulder and offer comfort. He resisted. They'd brought this on themselves. How different was this from the time he and his father had watched the Tsorians destroy Earth's meager forces? The fortunes of war, kid.

It seemed, however, that the ill fortune was expanding. The blue ships had now totally vanished from the sky, and in a ragged swarm the red ones were spreading southward over the sparkling city of San Francisco. Where they passed, the air quivered and flame began to rise. Within minutes most of the city seemed ablaze.

Jason watched, aghast. "They're destroying the City! They're destroying San Francisco! Why? Why are they doing that?"

From the darkness beside him, Aryl's voice was harsh. "They're Hykzoi."

"But . . . but we're not Tsorian!"

"Doesn't matter. Any client of their enemy is their enemy. Their policy is to make graphic examples of what happens to enemies."

She was silent a moment, then breathed in sharply. "San Francisco! Is that where you're holding my father?"

"No," Jason replied dully. "It's farther away."

"Then we must go there. He might still be able to get to the Fleet—if there's anything left of it."

"Shut up about your father, will you! What does he matter compared to this? Besides, I'm not allowed to take you."

She spun around and grabbed his shoulders, her claws just etching his skin. "Idiot! Can't you see how meaningless your games are now? What they're doing to that city, the Hykzoi could do to your whole world without a qualm."

"But I can't—"

"You must! Besides, those ships will very likely be here in a few minutes, giving this town the same treatment."

Jason looked again at the inferno across the Bay. Without a word, he turned and hurried down off the rocks, taking the easier route. Aryl kept close behind him. Up and down the street, people stood in front of their houses pointing and crying out.

Jason raced along the pavement. Any moment those horrified observers would realize what the Tsorian girl had just suggested. There'd be incredible panic and traffic jams.

He reached his mother's Chevy, parked innocently in front of the Morganthalls' house. Hurriedly he felt his pockets. No keys!

"Stay here!" he shouted to his unwelcome companion and sprinted up the stone stairs to the house. He hoped that in the streetlights, the neighbors wouldn't see the nature of that companion.

Once inside he charged upstairs to the room he'd been sleeping in and rummaged through several pants pockets until he found the keys. Next he ran into Professor Morganthall's study and grabbed the Colt .45 off the wall. It was the only weapon he'd seen in the house and was really only for display. He'd never seen any ammunition. But it looked the part, and no one need know it wasn't loaded. Good thing that Tsorian had lost her zapper, though he wished he'd gotten hold of it. No, he'd probably have ended up disintegrating himself.

He jammed the heavy gun into his jacket pocket, then bolted downstairs again, pausing only to grab a corner of the Indian-print tablecloth and tug, sending candlesticks and wooden fruit flying. Trailing the cloth behind him, he pelted back down to the car.

At first he thought Aryl had gone, but she was just standing in the shadow of a bush. Jason fumbled with the keys, opened the driver's side, and jumped in. He could drive off now and leave her on the sidewalk. But . . . well, maybe she could be useful.

He leaned across and unlocked the passenger door. As Aryl scrambled inside, he shoved the tablecloth at her. "Here, wrap up in this. Like a sari. If anyone sees you, maybe they'll think you're Indian or something."

"Why should I want to look Indian?"

Jason glared at her. "Because if you look like a Tsorian, people might tear you to pieces. Our world's getting blown apart, and your people brought it on us."

"The Hykzoi—"

"—wouldn't be here if it weren't for you! Now shut up, I've got to drive this thing."

He didn't want to mention that this was only the second time he'd driven alone. He jammed in the ignition key, turned it, and nothing happened. Then he remembered, grabbed the gear handle, and shifted into neutral. Again the key, and it started.

Slowly he moved down the street, trying to avoid the knots of terrified skygazers. Already, despite the hour, there were a growing number of cars on the roads. Soon there'd be panic, and if those red ships did move across the Bay, frenzied evacuation. Better avoid the main roads, he thought as he headed for the park route over the hills.

For a while they drove in silence, Jason concentrating on how the tree-hemmed road twisted and curved in the sweep of his headlights. Aryl just stared out at the steep slopes and the dark tangle of bushes and trees that reached out as they passed, almost trying to claw them from the road.

"How far is this place we're going?" she asked at last.

"About two hundred miles, maybe four hours' driving. We'll have to stop for gas somewhere."

Minutes more of silence went by. This was ridiculous, Jason thought. Here he was being forced to ride with this hateful alien, and he felt awkward about not keeping up a conversation. Still, he was a Resister agent. Maybe he could learn something useful. Besides, conversation would keep him from thinking about what he'd just seen.

"Did any of the others know you were coming here?"

"No." She kept looking out the window. "I don't matter much anymore. Oimog declared my father dead, and that stripped me of rank. I was a nonperson, but I had to try something."

Jason hadn't understood all of that, but he suspected she'd done something rather gutsy. "And you knew where to look for me because of what I'd said over dinner that time?"

"It was a wild gamble. I'd been hiding there since mid-day yesterday. I think I terrified a couple of little children who found me by accident. I was about ready to give up when you came."

The mountain road joined a freeway already filling with traffic. Conversation lapsed again. Jason wished it wouldn't. Pictures of the last hours kept rerunning through his head. Even the unfamiliarity of driving couldn't keep them away. He had stood on Indian Rock and in a few minutes watched the destruction of San Francisco. The City. How many times had he been there, visiting the zoo and museums, exploring Chinatown or shopping with his mother? How could it be gone? How could those hundreds of thousands of people be dead?

He wouldn't let himself get angry. If he did, he'd drive off the road, and he was having a hard enough time avoiding that as it was. Carefully taking one hand from the wheel, he switched on the radio and scanned the channels. Maybe there'd be music. But there was only static and hysterical announcers.

Everything on both sides of the Golden Gate was gone. San Francisco, Daly City, Sausalito, San Rafael. And of course, the Tsorian Headquarters had been blown away. Red ships sighted in various spots. Panic in East Bay cities, the governor of California appealing for calm. Calm, ha! The freeway was getting more crowded every moment.

"Those places they mentioned," Aryl said suddenly, "are they anywhere near—"

"No! Your precious father is perfectly safe! It's just a

few more of my cities that have been wiped out. Only a few hundred thousand more natives. Nothing important!"

"Oh, stop it! My base was destroyed too, you know, and my friends."

"But you're at war with those Hykzoi—we're not. They wouldn't be here at all if you hadn't tried to grab this planet for yourselves."

"Maybe that's so, but it can't be helped now. That's in the past. It's the future I'm worried about."

"Oh, so now San Francisco and the rest are just history and can be dismissed so you can get on with conquering other worlds."

"Don't be—"

"Tsorian, if you say one more word, I'm going to stop this car and throw you out. And you lost your fancy little gun, so I can do it too."

Aryl glared at him but said nothing more. Jason stared at the road. His cheek still smarted from the gashes she'd left there, and he wasn't at all sure he could actually manage to throw her out. But he did have his Colt .45. A bit primitive, maybe, but it could probably kill Tsorians well enough. If it were loaded.

They continued driving east with only the radio talking. Tsorian establishments around the world were being destroyed. Jason felt almost like cheering on the Hykzoi, except that nearby human towns were going at the same time. And besides, he had to admit to himself, what Aryl said was probably true. The Hykzoi seemed even worse than the Tsorians. At least the first lot of conquerors had never wiped out whole cities. Maybe they *were* slightly better devils. He kept his thoughts firmly to himself and drove.

The valley towns they drove through were obviously

awake, but here at least there was no mass panic. The stream of traffic they were flowing with was the first wave from the East Bay, and though most probably didn't know where they were going, they'd seen enough to want to go. Jason's hands ached from gripping the wheel, and his eyes burned from staring at the monotonous headlight-framed road.

They had crossed through the Central Valley and were climbing into the foothills when he decided they'd have to stop for gas. Normally most places would be closed at this hour, but there were lights on at Frank's Gas and Groceries and several cars parked out front. Jason pulled up to the self-serve pump and spoke to Aryl for the first time in miles.

"Wrap up in that tablecloth, will you? I don't want it to look like I'm transporting the enemy."

Jason got out and stuck the gas nozzle into the car's tank. The bells dinged steadily behind him. He glanced in the window to see Aryl flailing around with the tablecloth. She'd obviously never seen an Indian sari. She looked more like a paisley ghost.

When the tank was filled, Jason walked into the store to pay, glad his mother had left him the credit card and a wad of cash. Maybe he'd better buy something to eat while he was at it. He hadn't even realized he was hungry until he saw the rows of junk food. What sort of snacks did Tsorians eat? Well, she'd eat what he bought or go hungry.

Hurriedly he picked out a bag of potato chips, two cans of root beer, and a bunch of bananas. Then his eye fell on one of those mosquito nets campers wear over their heads when the bugs get really bad. That might help his passenger's disguise.

He approached the checkout counter where a group of

men were huddled around a sputtering radio and trading rumors.

"Well, I'm surprised that if things are that bad, we haven't had more folks through here by now," the check-out man was saying as he rang up Jason's purchases. "You'd think everyone in the Bay Area would hightail it for the mountains."

"Give'em another half hour," another man commented. "Though why the mountains'll be any safer I don't know."

"Hell, man, it's obvious," said another. "It's big cities they're picking off. Cities here, a couple in Europe, one even in China, I heard."

"They can have those places, but San Francisco—well, that's something else."

"And San Jose. I heard that's gone, too. If I could just get my hands on those purple bastards!"

"I thought it was some other bunch."

"Nah. They're all the same."

Jason had to fight not to join in and straighten them out. But hadn't he been saying pretty much the same thing to Aryl? Better just get going.

He grabbed up his bag of groceries and stuffed the mosquito net into his pocket. Suddenly there was a commotion from outside, and everyone's head turned to the door. A burly man forced his way through struggling with a snarling creature in a paisley cloth. Black eyes flashed angrily under a tousle of pale gray hair.

twelve

ARYL HAD ONLY STEPPED OUT OF THE CAR FOR A MINUTE. She'd finally given up trying to wrap herself in that ridiculous cloth while sitting inside a cramped metal box. Struggling to check her costuming in the side mirror, she'd just gotten the shroud to look reasonable, though she'd make no guarantees about authenticity, when a native thug grabbed her out of the darkness. He started shouting rude things at her and dragging her toward the building. After she'd nearly ripped his eye out with her free hand, he wrenched both arms behind her back and pushed her roughly through the door.

"Boys, look what I caught!" he bawled as he struggled to keep hold of her wrists. "One of those murdering purple devils was actually skulking around in the parking lot. Nearly gouged my eye out, but I caught it."

Aryl stared about the murderous looking crowd and saw Jason standing in the back looking stunned and ashen faced. No help there. Suddenly someone yanked away most of the enveloping cloth and whistled, "And a female, too!"

"Well, isn't that nice." Another man placed a meaty hand on her shoulder, and Aryl promptly sank her needle-sharp teeth into it. He howled with rage and raised his good hand to strike her.

"Hold on!" someone else said. "Maybe we can find out from her why all this is happening."

"Who cares *why*," came a reply. "It's *what* that counts. They've killed thousands of human beings."

"They have not!" Jason pushed forward, suddenly, surprised to find himself staring at a ring of angry faces. He avoided even glancing at Aryl but forged ahead. "Her people haven't done it; it's those people in the red ships. The Hykzoi. They're the Tsorians' enemies too."

"So how come you know so much about these space people, kid?" said the man with the bleeding hand. "You a collaborator?"

"No! I'm not. I just don't like to see someone blamed for something they haven't done."

"Red ships, blue ships, what's the difference? Her people have enough to answer for anyway."

The man who was holding Aryl now peered around at Jason. "Hey, you came with her in that green Chevy, didn't you?"

Aryl stared as Jason slid a hand into his pocket and pulled out a large, evil-looking native weapon. "Yes, I did. And I'm going to leave with her in it right now."

Apparently, Aryl realized, this was a weapon to take seriously, because everyone stepped back a pace or two. With one more vicious twist, the man holding Aryl suddenly let go. She'd begun rubbing her sore wrists when Jason firmly grabbed her arm and started backing through the door.

The screen had barely slammed behind them when they both turned and raced for the car.

Aryl caught part of the still-trailing tablecloth in the

door but just left it hanging out as Jason gunned the engine and they lurched out of the parking lot. She twisted around to look out the window and saw men pouring out of the building and into cars. Then the rear window shattered. With a sharp crack something seemed to strike into it.

"Jeez, they're shooting at us!" Jason exclaimed as he pushed down the accelerator even harder.

"That was a gunshot?" she asked incredulously, then an angry frown crossed her face. "Well, hand me that weapon of yours. I'll see if I can shoot them back."

Jason shook his head. "Can't! It's not loaded."

She stared at him. "You threatened all those people with a nonfunctional weapon?"

"They didn't know that." He shot an anxious look at the side mirror. "Scrunch down below the seat, will you? It looks like the whole posse is after us."

Aryl did as he suggested, glad that this way she couldn't see the bends they were veering around. Jason was driving like a lunatic, and there seemed to be an awfully steep drop on the right side.

What sounded like another shot whizzed past them. She inched over and peered out at the side mirror. A chain of headlights was speeding along after them. These people were all lunatics. Another shot seemed to miss them too.

Suddenly Jason began struggling with the wheel. "A flat! They must have hit a tire!" His next comment turned into a startled yell as the car suddenly veered sideways, bucked off the road, and began careening down the slope.

Aryl stared in openmouthed horror at the trees bouncing by them. Right in the path of their jolting headlights one very large tree was coming closer and closer.

Frantically she fought with the door until it burst open.

Then she sank a set of claws into Jason's shoulder, yanked him out from behind the wheel, and hurled herself and him out of the car.

The ground was hard and covered with sharp jabbing things, but eventually it seemed to stop moving. She lay on it listening to the receding crashing sounds until they were replaced by a tearing thud, then an explosion. She threw an arm over her face to ward off the light. A wave of heat singed her hair and skin.

Slowly the inferno died into a mere fire, and cautiously Aryl sat up. Jason was lying on his stomach a few feet from her.

"Thanks," he said through a mouthful of dirt. "I needed that." Then to her surprise he actually laughed. "Do you realize you still have that tablecloth attached to you?"

She looked down and saw one end of the offending cloth still tucked into her belt. The rest splayed over the slope behind her. She tried to dislodge it, but Jason, who was just sitting up, said, "No, keep it. You obviously need all the disguise you can get."

Very shakily he stood up. "If you can walk, we'd better split before the highway patrol or someone comes to investigate. Our pursuers have obviously decided they weren't involved."

Aryl figured he was talking so much because he was surprised to be alive, but she was still so shaken she wasn't sure she could talk at all. She wanted to say something scathing about primitive native cars, but stopped as she remembered seeing a number of her own advanced strike-ships shot down just a few hours earlier.

In silence she stumbled to her feet, checked that everything still seemed to be working, and followed Jason down the steep slope. It was slippery with a carpet of long, thin, almost needlelike leaves that must have fallen from this forest of trees. She kept tripping over the wretched trailing cloth until she stopped and looped it around an arm.

The only light came from the still-burning car, and gradually it too fell behind. She had to walk carefully to avoid smashing into the rough trunks of trees. They were everywhere, dark and hostile. Only the downward slope and the sound of Jason crashing on ahead gave her any sense of where she was going.

Suddenly the horrid trees were behind her and she found herself stumbling onto a flat, hard surface. She stood still, trying to orient herself in the dark. "Where is this?"

"A road. Hey, maybe it's the old highway!"

"Is that good?"

"Yeah. We ought to be able to follow it north until it joins with the new highway. There were some stretches where there wasn't a better route for building the new one."

"So which way is north?"

"Look at the stars."

She did. Over the road, with the trees cleared back, there was a stretch of open sky. But the stars were few and meaningless. Apparently, however, they were not meaningless to her companion.

"There's the Big Dipper, so that other must be the North Star. This way," Jason announced.

Aryl turned and tromped after him, her boots making a far more decisive sound on the hard surface than his soft native shoes. She felt far from decisive. The excitement of their escape was dying away, and she was tired, cold, and hungry. The only thing she could do about any of that was to wrap the thin tablecloth around her like a cloak and keep going. She was determined not to be the first to stop.

Several times they had to duck behind trees or scramble up rocky banks to hide from approaching cars. But at least the jouncing headlights gave them plenty of warning.

Mostly they trudged in silence, though once Jason muttered, "Wish I hadn't lost all the food I bought. All I got out of that stop was a new mosquito net and enough gas to immolate my mother's car."

Aryl at least shared his first wish. She could have eaten anything, no matter what planet it grew on.

Above them, the tree-bordered ribbon of sky began to lighten, until not even the brightest of the unfamiliar stars could be seen. Aryl plodded on, vaguely surprised that her feet, which had long since become too cold to feel, could still move. Then, a chink of light appeared through the tall, straight tree trunks to her right. The planet's sun, a bright, warm, golden light. Maybe she wouldn't die of cold after all.

She walked on almost in a trance, aware only of the sun's growing warmth. Suddenly she ran right into Jason. He had stopped in the middle of the road in front of her.

He grunted but didn't even object. "It's no good. I've got to stop and get some rest. I'm a walking zombie."

Aryl didn't know what that was but figured it probably described her as well. She wasn't even up to pretending that Tsorians could endure more than humans.

"Let's find someplace hidden off the road," he said, pointing vaguely up a forested slope, "and take a nap. Just a short one." Jason scrambled up the bank, and fighting bushes, Aryl stumbled along behind. She found him again standing in a clump of small young trees and one tall, daunting one, which together screened a rocky hollow from the road.

Aryl chose a spot less rocky than others and gratefully

sank to the ground. It was covered with those strange pointy leaves. Their odor was pungent and highly alien, but at this point she hardly cared. She rustled around, trying to make herself comfortable, then after a moment's hesitation, unwrapped the tablecloth from her shoulders and offered half of it to Jason. Sleepily he nodded and tugged a portion over himself.

The last thing Aryl remembered before sinking into sleep was the harsh call of some native animal in the trees above her. She hoped it wasn't large and carnivorous, because she was far too exhausted to fight it off.

thirteen

JASON AWAKENED TO THE NOISE OF FURIOUS CHATTERING. He opened his eyes and stared into black, beady ones. Not a Tsorian, a squirrel. It hung upside down on a tree trunk not five feet from him, waving its bushy tail and regaling him with a torrent of abuse.

He heard a rustling beside him in the thicket. Aryl was curled up tightly, studying the squirrel. "Is it dangerous, or just nasty tempered?"

"Just telling us that this is its patch of trees. We earthlings are very territorial, you know."

She didn't answer. Giving the squirrel an unmistakably rude gesture, she sat up and began brushing pine needles off herself. Jason turned away, then forced himself to say what he knew he had to. "I really didn't thank you properly for pulling me out of that car last night."

"Then we're even. I didn't thank you for getting me away from those vicious maniacs."

Jason felt he had to defend his fellow humans. "Oh, they probably weren't all that bad a bunch—if they hadn't been dealing with a Tsorian. You people have built up a lot of resentment for yourselves, you know, even if most humans aren't actively involved in the Resistance."

Aryl opened her mouth then closed it again. She looked down at her hands. "Yes, my father's told me how poorly this occupation was being run."

"And like a good Tsorian, you believe that, because your daddy says it, it's true."

"No!" she snapped. "I believe it because it seems to *be* true. And don't you ridicule the parent/child relationship. You haven't the faintest concept of what that should be."

Jason's anger flared, though he knew his comment hadn't been very fair. "I do too, so shut up! Do you think I'd be going through all this just to take you to your precious father? Even if he could turn this war of yours around? You forget, my mother's up there too."

Aryl began an angry reply, then stopped herself. She turned away with what Jason thought was almost a laugh. "And if she's as thick-headed as you, they've probably been spending the last few weeks yelling at each other just like this. Let's get going."

The sun was well up now, though it still seemed to be morning, and the cold had been replaced by a dry, dusty heat. Scraggly manzanita and sagebrush shared the slopes with tall pines and with rounded granite boulders, their rough surfaces glinting with flecks of mica. A fine day for a mountain hike, Jason thought, though he was hardly in the mood for one. He wanted to be at that cabin *now*. In the meantime, he wouldn't mind something to eat or drink.

It seemed that Tsorian bodies worked much like human bodies. In a few minutes Aryl said, "I don't suppose any of this stuff growing around here is good to eat?"

"Not for humans, for deer maybe. I don't know about Tsorians. But why don't we stop at the next cabin we see and beg some food? After all, we are refugees." He looked at her, noting that the dust had only slightly lightened her maroon complexion. "I'll do the begging."

There were few cars to dodge on the road that morning, but it wasn't long before they saw a cabin tucked back in the woods. Jason had Aryl wait behind a boulder while he walked up the dusty drive and knocked at the door. There was no answer. Then he noticed that the windows were all shuttered and pine needles and cones were scattered thickly over the porch. A summer cabin still closed up. Discouraged, he turned back to see that Aryl had come up behind him.

"What's the matter? No one at home?"

"The place hasn't been opened for the season yet."

"Maybe they left some food behind."

"Well, maybe some canned things. But I'm not going to break in and—"

"*You* don't have to. I'm the evil conqueror, remember? And I'm also starving." She pushed past him and examined the doorknob and lock. Spreading out her three fingers, she slid claws in at the appropriate places and tugged. There was a rending crack, and in moments the whole assembladge was wrenched free of the door.

Jason was impressed and couldn't hide it. "Doesn't hurt to have your ever-ready tool kit along."

The door had just swung open into cool darkness when a sound from above drew their attention back outside. They looked up through the pine branches, then instantly flattened themselves against the outside wall. Three glowing red rings disappeared over the trees. Gradually the thrumming in the air faded.

"Where would they be heading?" Aryl asked tensely.

"Unless they're into casino gambling, there's not much

to attract them up that way. No cities or anything, unless
. . ."

"Unless?"

Jason couldn't miss the anguish in her face. "Unless maybe they've found out where they can pick up an enemy commander."

Like a shot, Aryl was off the porch and running along the road in the direction the ships had taken. Jason forgot about being hungry. "Hey, wait! You can't run all that way. We've still got to make it to the new highway. Then we can try to hitch a ride."

When he finally caught up with her, Aryl's face was even more powdered with dust, but she still looked far from human. "Stop a moment, will you? If we're going to hitch, you've got to do the foreign student routine again."

"I will not wrap up in that beastly cloth!"

"Do you want another reception like the one at the gas station?"

She scowled, but unslung the cloth from her shoulders and started enshrouding herself in it. Jason couldn't believe the mess she was making. He had to help.

Finally she was wrapped to Jason's satisfaction. With the addition of the mosquito netting over her face, he thought she looked a little like those ladies in the *National Geographic* from Yemen or someplace.

The two set off again with the occasional grumble from Aryl about how hot, dusty, and blind she was. When, after an hour's hike, they at last reached the intersection of the old and new highways, Jason said, "Now remember, keep your face down and your hands tucked in the cloth. You're supposed to be a submissive female." He could almost feel the laser glare from her veiled black eyes.

From where they stood on a wide shoulder of the road,

they could see that the traffic was much heavier now as refugees streamed into the mountains. But even as they watched, it seemed that traffic flowing the other way was picking up as well.

Jason walked closer to the pavement, stood firmly, and began waving his thumb at passing cars. Nobody stopped. He felt extremely uncomfortable doing what a lifetime of admonitions had warned him not to. But then, he thought wryly, if some mugger picked them up, Aryl could tear his face off.

Glancing at his companion, he saw with alarm that she was imitating his hitchhiking gesture. "Hey, leave this to me!" he shouted over the rumble of traffic. "Someone might notice your purple thumb."

Grumbling, Aryl folded her arms in her paisley robes and went back to standing with downcast face the way Jason imagined some demure Yemeni might. He would have laughed if he weren't afraid of setting off her temper again.

It seemed they'd been standing there begging for hours when a big semi slowed and pulled over. The driver leaned toward the open window on the passenger's side. "Where you two headed?"

"Lake Tahoe," Jason replied eagerly.

"East side or west?"

"Eh . . . east."

"Well, I'm going up the west side, but I can take you as far as the 'Y.' Hop in."

They scrambled up into the high cab, Jason deliberately placing himself next to the driver. "Thanks a lot. It didn't look as if anyone was going to stop."

"Yeah, they've all got their wind up about the space people. As I see it, you can't second-guess what those creatures'll do, so you might as well go about your business as usual. You two Bay Area refugees?"

Jason nodded and decided he'd try to be as truthful as he could. "Yes. My friend and I were heading up to my uncle's cabin when we had a flat on the old highway and drove off the road. The car's totaled, so we decided to try and hitch. Eh . . . she's from Yemen, an exchange student."

"I wondered. Don't normally pick up hitchhikers, but you two looked too interesting to pass up."

As the truck's radio droned through the pause, Jason hoped this guy wouldn't find out how right he was. Suddenly Aryl spoke up. Jason tensed, but decided the driver probably couldn't tell a Yemeni accent from a Tsorian one.

"Your radio, has it mentioned any spaceships up ahead?"

"Yep. It reported something going on around Stateline. Think you're heading from the frying pan to the fire, eh?"

Cold fear spread through Jason. Uncle Carl's cabin wasn't too far from Stateline.

"So, anyway," the driver said around the wad of gum he was chewing, "did you two see what happened in the Bay Area? Tell me about it. I was coming up through Fresno."

Jason didn't want to think about it, much less talk about it. Still, this was a way to pay for the lift. He tried to report like a passive observer, but putting it into words was like reliving the whole thing. All those cities, he thought to himself, all those people, destroyed in a callous instant by these new invaders. Somehow he didn't think there'd be any point to joining a Resistance against *them*. He wondered if there had really been any even against the Tsorians. What good had all their meetings and planning and little rebellions done except make life harder or shorter for some people and make the Resisters imagine that they weren't quite as powerless as they really were? Finally his account to the driver, minus all the personal stuff, ran down.

For a minute the man said nothing, then he let out his breath in a throaty sigh. "That must've been something to see—and have lived through. It's hard to believe. Frisco. I was just there last week. Whew! I sure as hell hope those little red ships haven't been at this everywhere. Though the stuff I've been getting over the radio's so garbled I can't tell what's happening."

Aryl spoke quietly, her voice muffled by the netting. "Surely there is only a danger near where Tsorians have facilities."

"Well, maybe. But in that case there must've been some of those purple guys up ahead doing the casinos. Notice how the traffic coming this way has picked up? Everybody's driving like they're crazy scared too."

Jason felt as if he'd been shaken awake. For the first time in nearly an hour, he noticed things going on outside his head. Traffic was pelting down from the direction they were heading, and some of their own stream of traffic seemed to be turning around. Everywhere there was honking, swerving chaos.

"You're not turning back, are you?" he asked in alarm.

"Nah. Got to be in Denver in twenty-four hours. But I can't say I like this. Hey, miss." The driver leaned forward and peered at Aryl. "You see many of these space people in Yemen?"

"I have seen a great many of them, yes."

"Never thought much about them really, not after they first forced their way in, that is. Oh, I'd as soon they'd left us alone or at least done something helpful if they was set

113

on meddling. But I just figured they was here to stay, so I might as well accept it. Didn't affect me none anyhow. But now . . . Well, if this's how our future's going to be, I don't much care for it."

"Neither do I," she said quietly. "I truly hope it is not."

Finally, like fish swimming upstream, they made their way to the highway junction. The truck driver let them out with admonitions to take care. Jason watched him drive off, feeling suddenly very much alone.

"Guess we walk from here," he said gruffly. "It's not too many more miles, and it sure doesn't look like we'll catch many lifts going this way."

They began trudging mechanically along the highway, past pine trees mingled with shopping centers, fast-food places, and motels. Some of those spots had been meadows or woods when Jason had first started coming to Uncle Carl's cabin in the summer. Those had been golden times that he'd treasured year after year. And always the drive up had been filled with anticipation, each special landmark showing they were a little closer: a certain rock formation that looked like a face, a waterfall you had to crane your neck to see, an old rustic restaurant with plastic gnomes in front. This trip, his mind had been so torn up he hadn't noticed any of them.

But what he did notice now was that the passing traffic was lessening. The parking lots of the motels were almost empty. Everywhere there was an eerie Sunday-morning quiet. He tried not to see these ominous signs and instead watched as he always had for the occasional flash of blue through the trees on his left as the highway ran closer and closer to the lake. That great sheet of water looked calm and untroubled. He wished he could absorb some of that.

Suddenly they were there. On the left, the shops and

motels ended, replaced by a Cyclone fence that protected an old enclave of summer cabins. He stopped so suddenly at the gate that Aryl bumped into him, blurting out what sounded like a Tsorian curse. He'd heard quite a few as she'd stumbled along in her entangling tablecloth.

"In here," he said, heading down the rutted dirt road. The gate, usually latched, was swinging wide open. A few yards inside, and the trees engulfed them in quiet. Dark, tall trees, unbearably heavy with the tang of pine. Everything seemed unchanged.

Here and there, drives branched off to cabins in the woods. Mailboxes were marked with family names, and he knew each one. Browning, Clark, Effingham, Gish. All part of the summer lore. Baseball games, campfires, fearless explorations in the woods.

The band of trees came to an end, and he hesitated to step from their calming shade. Before him stretched the meadow, tall grass, wind-rippled and gleaming in the late-afternoon sun. Insects hummed in the air and the occasional blackbird rose with a warbling call and a flash of ebony and scarlet. It almost seemed normal. Almost.

Something unsettling hung in the air, an odd metallic stench. And there was no one about. It was early in the season, but still there should be a few vacationers and certainly some of the year-round residents.

Fearfully Jason walked forward, Aryl close and silent behind him. Here the dirt road was thick with the usual soft, pale dust. It plopped up around his feet. Automatically Jason sidestepped around a run-over frog left flat in the road, thin and dry as paper. He used to think these things were neat, but now he ignored it just as he ignored the live frogs plishing through the grasses into the swampy water. His eyes were on a hazy pall in the air ahead. The stench was getting stronger.

Finally he saw what was different. The haze hung over a large patch of meadow where green had been turned to scorched black. Fear mounted as he hurried forward.

On the far side of the meadow stretched the trees and cabins that bordered the lake. Only the usual picture was broken. Two clumps of trees stood like black, naked skeletons. In a wide space between them, there was nothing. There should have been more trees, there should have been a cabin. But there was nothing. Only a clear, unobstructed view of the lake, as if something huge had come along and chomped out a section of shoreline. The section where Uncle Carl's cabin had stood.

Jason just stood and stared, while behind him, Aryl started to say something, then stopped. Slowly she unwrapped herself from her disguise and let it fall into the dust. She turned away and looked toward the blue, pine-clad mountains.

Jason's stupor was ripped by a voice. "Heaven above! Jason Sikes! Why, that's you, isn't it? Come on over here!"

Jason stared and couldn't believe what he saw. One of the Bentson sisters. Gertrude he thought; yes, the thin one. The two batty old ladies lived there all year round next to his uncle's cabin—or former cabin. Were they still there, with this happening next door?

Slowly he walked toward the beckoning figure, her flowery peasant dress draped with turquoise necklaces.

"Jason, dear dear boy," she said, giving him a quick bony hug as soon as he was within reach. "Rather a poor start to a vacation this year, isn't it?"

"Eh, yes . . . Miss Gertrude . . ."

The woman's eyes widened under her tousled mop of

gray hair as she looked over Jason's shoulder. "And you've brought a girlfriend this year, how nice. One of them I see, but no matter. Times change, times change. How do you do, dear. I'm Gertrude Bentson. And you are . . . ?"

"Oh. I am Aryl."

"A nice name, really. Why don't you two come inside. Emily will be back soon. She drove out to the store, and also to spy around a little and see what's cooking, I dare say. Quite a to-do."

Jason felt totally bemused as he followed Miss Bentson into the front room of the little cabin. Briefly he looked around at the familiar knotty-pine walls, the Indian rugs, the shelves of china birds and pinecone art. "Miss Gertrude," he ventured, "could you tell us what happened next door?"

"Yes, yes. Have a seat," she said, pointing to a couple of rattan rockers by the fireplace. She plumped up a pillow on another chair and settled into it. "It was really quite something. Just a few hours ago, and it all happened so fast. Emily and I could scarcely believe it. A bad business all around."

"Yes, but what happened?"

"Well, we were hanging out our washing. We'd spent most of the morning doing it and had two baskets full. The people in your uncle's cabin were puttering about as usual. Been there several weeks, they had, and I hadn't seen most of them before, except your mother, of course, Jason. Didn't see much of her, though, this visit, but then they had that special guest, so I expect she was busy."

"Special guest?" Aryl said tensely.

The woman smiled at her. "Yes, do you know him? One of your people, I believe. Such a handsome man, once you

117

get used to the skin color, and such striking gray hair. Emily says I'm always a pushover for distinguished-looking gray hair. She likes blonds, Emily does. But we didn't really get a chance to meet him. Kept inside most of the time he did, except that recently in the evenings some of them would go out and sit on the beach."

"But what about this morning?" Jason prompted impatiently.

"Oh, yes, this morning. It was awful, really. We were hanging out the laundry, Emily and I, when this great big red belt buckle came dropping out of the sky. It wasn't a belt buckle, of course, just shaped like one, a red one. But it was making this awful kind of a noise that gets into your ears and wants to burst right out again. It came down out of the sky and landed right in the meadow. Shocking thing! It could have started a big fire if the grasses hadn't been so wet."

"And then . . . ?" Jason urged, but the sound of a car engine interrupted.

"Oh, good, there's Emily back from the store. She's much better at telling things than I am." As the sputtering motor came to a stop, Gertrude bustled out, and Aryl leaned toward Jason.

"Is this woman quite normal?"

"Not in the least, but she's harmless. Her sister's the less batty of the two, so maybe we can get some answers."

Chattering happily, Gertrude, now clutching a bag of groceries, ushered her sister in. "Isn't it nice they could come and visit, Emily? I've been telling them about this morning, but you're so much better at this sort of thing. Why don't you try? I'd just gotten to where the belt buckle landed in the meadow. What a mess, too. All that scorched grass won't grow back for a year."

After effusively greeting her guests, plump, white-haired Emily plunked herself down on a worn flower-patterned couch and took up the tale.

"Of course Gertrude and I were somewhat alarmed, so we hid behind the boathouse and watched. And I tell you, the things that came out of there were worth being alarmed about. They looked sort of like big jackknives with lots of blades.

"Well, it was all crazy after that. People in the cabin were shooting at them, and the jackknives were shooting back, only they didn't use bullets. They had flashlight things, but the light made people fall down as good as bullets."

Aryl drew in her breath. "What color was the light . . . eh, Miss Emily?"

"Red, dear, like Christmas."

"Yes, but could you tell me what shade of red? It's very important."

"Well, now, you're right. Red's a lot of different colors, isn't it? Now let's see. Help me, Gertrude, what shade of red was it?"

"It wasn't really a fire-engine red, not a fuchsia either. Really more like salmon, I'd say."

"Yes"—Emily nodded—"or coral."

Aryl looked completely baffled. Anxiously, Jason stood up and walked to a sideboard. "Maybe you could point out the color here. There's lots of different shades in this china."

"What a clever boy! Yes, indeed." Emily popped up and waddled to the sideboard. "Let's see, I'd say it was like this."

"More like on the pitcher, I'd say, Emily."

"Yes, Gertrude's right. Just the shade of this petunia here."

Aryl looked at the soft orange-pink of the flower and let out a sigh of relief. "Then they didn't mean to kill them."

"I don't know what they meant to do, but I'm sure they *did* kill at least one of them."

Aryl and Jason tensed up, simultaneously asking, "Who?"

"The one with the big belly and the brown beard. I don't know his name, but he'd been staying there the whole time. As soon as those jackknives showed up, he ran outside and began shouting that he was the one who'd contacted them and they should . . . what was it he said . . . ? Ah, yes, they should negotiate with him. He had helped them win their war, and now he had some demands. Strange, wasn't it?"

"Jerry Barns," Jason said, understanding slowly falling into place.

"What?" Aryl whispered.

"Jerry Barns. He was always arguing that we should sell Rogav to the Hykzoi in exchange for a better deal from their empire."

"Oh, dear," Emily interrupted, "I hope he wasn't a friend of yours, because the jackknives turned their flashlights on him. A very dark red that time."

"Yes," Gertrude put in. "Almost fuchsia."

"And it blew him quite apart."

They all were silent a moment, then Aryl whispered, "And what happened to the others in the cabin?"

"Well, I'm not sure how many there were in the first place. But three of them were dragged out and put in the red round thing. A spaceship, I guess it was."

"Which three?" Jason asked.

"Your mother was one, dear, and there was a man I

120

didn't know, the bald one. And then there was the space gentleman Gertrude was so taken with. Then all the jack-knives scurried back on board, and the thing zipped way up in the air and shot a big bright flashlight beam down on the cabin. It just went up in a puff. Never seen anything like it. Just left some charred ground and a few dead trees. I must say, it dried our laundry quick as anything."

Jason rocked back on his chair, a little dazed. "And then what happened?"

"Oh, it joined two other red ring things. They shot off north and disappeared.

Aryl sighed like a punctured balloon. Her voice quavered. "Well, that's the end, then."

"Not really," Gertrude added. "They didn't go very far. When I was out at the store, there was quite a fuss because those spaceships had flown over Stateline and landed among those new condominiums up by the cove. Everybody was tearing out of there. I mean, spaceships landing in your front yard is not what you expect when you buy into a place like that. At Stateline people were pouring out of the casinos too and just taking off. The place was in an uproar. The police, poor things, were way over their heads."

"They landed by some condominiums?" Jason asked incredulously.

"Yes, you know, the big, expensive new ones four or five miles beyond Stateline. The ones with the putting green in the middle. What's it called? Lake something. That's no good; they're all called Lake something around here. Lake View Retreat. That's it."

Jason jumped up. "Then there's still a chance! Come on, Aryl, we've got to go there."

"Oh, you can't go there, dear," Emily said. "The police have got it all cordoned off. Not that anyone wants to go there. There was talk about how those red ship people had turned beams on some of the residents there, and they just blew apart like the poor fellow here."

"But still, we do have to go there," Aryl said as she stood up.

"Oh, dear," Gertrude said, wringing her hands. "Whyever for? It sounds terribly dangerous to me."

"Don't be silly, Gertrude," her sister snapped. "They want to try to rescue those poor people. But it would be terribly dangerous to go by road, even if you could get past the police."

Jason frowned. "Then . . . then we'll go by water. Do you still have that old wooden canoe I used to borrow?"

"The *Lady of the Lake*!" Gertrude said, jumping up and clapping her hands. "Yes, we do, and they could borrow it, couldn't they, Emily? A rescue mission, how exciting! But you really should wait until after dark. It's almost sunset now, see!" She bustled to the crocheted curtains and pulled them back. The sun was hanging heavy and gold just above the purpled mountains on the far side of the lake. The flat, glassy water rippled a golden path across its surface to wash up wave by wave on the sand.

"Yes, you should wait," Emily said, standing up. "And what's more, I want you to have a good meal before you go, and a little rest. I can see that you both look absolutely done in."

Jason chafed at the delay, but the mention of food suddenly reminded him of how hungry he was. And he couldn't deny that he was feeling all swimmy headed from lack of sleep. He looked at Aryl, and she nodded wearily.

"All right, we'll wait a little. But I want to be off before midnight."

"Midnight!" Gertrude breathed. "Oh, how exciting!"

✤ f o u r t e e n ✤

ARYL WAS SURE SHE'D NEVER GET ANY SLEEP. NOT AFTER all she'd just heard and all that heavy alien food. And certainly not in this uncomfortable alien bed, with those two bizarre women about. But the next thing she knew, one of those women was shaking her out of a profound, exhausted sleep.

"Nearly midnight, dearie, time to get up!" Gertrude said cheerily. "My, I think you do have lovely hair. It's really a splendid idea to have young people with gray hair. That would get rid of a lot of ageism, don't you think?"

Aryl mumbled something groggily as she climbed out of the too soft bed. She was fully dressed; she'd been too tired even to take off her boots.

"And your eyes," the woman continued as she bustled around the room. "They look like the eyes of those little chipmunks who come visit us when we have breakfast on the patio. It's too bad you'll be leaving before they arrive. I'm certain you'd get along splendidly."

Aryl was far less certain about that. What had Jason called these women? Batty? She didn't know the term, but its meaning was becoming more and more clear.

While they'd slept, the ladies had prepared a huge picnic

123

hamper, which they now thrust on the two children. Then they all four tromped out to the boat shed and dragged out the long, white canoe.

Aryl stared at it, aghast. It didn't look as if it could even float, let alone take them anywhere.

Jason was also shaking his head. "I don't know if a *white* canoe is the best vehicle for stealth."

"Nonsense, dear," Emily replied. "It'll blend in with the moonlight on the water. Besides, those jackknife people probably won't be expecting an amphibious assault, so to speak."

"One if by land and two if by sea!" Gertrude intoned happily.

With difficulty the four of them hauled the heavy wooden boat down to the water. Finally they had its prow edged into the silver-fringed wavelets that rippled onto the wet sand.

"Now, Jason," Emily said, "better take off your sneakers before you wade out there. Your mother'd never forgive me if I let you go running about rescuing her in wet shoes. You'd better take yours off too, dear. Those are such nice boots."

Aryl didn't feel like arguing. Besides, her feet had been screaming to get out of those boots for hours. Struggling to pull them off, she tossed them into the boat. The sand curling up between her clawed toes was cool and wonderfully soft. She sighed with relief.

Then she noticed Jason staring at her feet and would have been offended if she hadn't been so busy staring at his. Ugly, pale, stubby-looking things. And with five toes!

The women didn't seem to be paying attention to either set of feet. "I'll just put the hamper in the center of the boat," Emily said. "And you both must wear your life jackets, you know. It's one of our little rules."

Jason deftly fastened the straps on his own jacket then helped Aryl as she was struggling with hers. "Do you know how to swim?" he whispered.

"Of course!" Her objection lost some of its indignation at the first slap of stinging cold water against her bare feet. She'd always enjoyed swimming, but in water a good deal warmer. This was liquid ice.

Jason waded out, pulling the prow of the boat partway into the water. "All right, you climb in and walk carefully to the front. Sit facing outward. Careful! Stay in the center or you'll tip the whole thing over."

The boat rocked violently under her as Aryl tried to walk its length. What an impossible way to travel! Finally she stepped over the little woven seat and, causing one last lurch, sat facing out into the lake.

Jason gave a final push. The stern ground over the sand, then suddenly was floating free. Quickly Jason hopped aboard. He called and waved farewells to the Bentson sisters as the boat shot smoothly into the dark lake.

Aryl felt sudden panic—and exhilaration. She was completely exposed. Overhead stretched the vastness of the universe. It gleamed with cold and silence and with frightening alien stars. Beneath her and on all sides stretched a life-quelling emptiness almost as awesome. And yet she, in this frail shell of a boat, had the audacity to venture between them. She felt small and insignificant—a very un-Tsorian sensation.

Her reverie was shattered as something jabbed into her back. "Here's your paddle. I'm not propelling a pleasure barge, you know."

"You're not expected to," she said, indignantly grabbing the wooden device and digging it into the water. The boat rocked violently.

"Wait! Let me show you. Put one hand on top. No, the other one. Right. Now grip the shaft farther down with the other hand. Hmm, your arms don't seem to bend in quite the right way. Well, it ought to work. Then dip the blade in. No, so it's at an angle to the boat's side. That's right, dip and pull it back through the water. Lift it out and bring it forward. Good. Again."

The instruction continued, with Aryl surprised at how swiftly words produced a pattern, a pattern that worked and propelled them smoothly forward. When, with her paddling in front and Jason behind, she finally felt comfortable enough to look away from the rhythmic motion of her paddle, she was astonished to see how far they'd come. The cabin they'd left was only a tiny speck of light on a dark, receding shore.

Again she felt the yawning emptiness, but it was tempered by beauty. To her left, the planet's waxing moon cast a glimmering, rippling path of silver. It sloshed right up against the boat, and when she paddled on that side, the water dripping from the raised blade looked like jewels. The noise of that splashing and the gentle slap of water on the prow were the only sounds in a vast silence.

She hated to break that silence. But they were on a mission. "All right, I'm paddling. Where do we go?"

"That's not your problem, the steering's done back here. This old-fashioned wooden canoe weighs a ton, but it handles really well in the water—as long as novices don't gyrate around too much."

"Well, I've never been in a craft as primitive as this before."

"Don't knock it. It's getting us where we're going, isn't

it?" He was quiet a moment, then said more softly, "Aryl, do you . . . do you think they're still alive?"

She fought down fear before she could answer. "They must be. A beam of that shade would only have incapacitated them. Hykzoi usually don't take prisoners, but my father's value to them is obvious, either as a hostage or . . . or as someone to extract information from. If natives were found near a Tsorian commander, the Hykzoi would probably assume they had some significance as well. They obviously know little of the local situation."

In the darkness, Jason scowled at the arrogance of that remark, then he shrugged. "But why would they take them only as far as Lake View Retreat?"

"The only thing I can think of is that there's still a battle raging out there." Aryl gestured at the star-sprinkled blackness overhead. "They may think it's not safe yet to transfer important prisoners to one of their battleships. But we don't know how long that will last. We must hurry."

"If you can paddle faster, do."

Aryl stiffled a groan. Her shoulder muscles were already telling her that this sort of movement was something she was not designed for. But in a moment, her attention was fixed elsewhere.

"What's that? Are we nearing our goal?"

"That glow there? Heck no, that's just Stateline. I can't believe they're still at it. Space marauders camped a few miles away, and those neon-lit casinos are still going full tilt."

"What are casinos?"

"Places where people go to gamble. You know, putting out money for the chance of making more. It's legal in

Nevada but not in California, so where the states join, a lot of casinos are built to lure California gamblers."

"Then that makes sense."

"What?"

"Those people staying around with the Hykzoi nearby. It's just another form of gambling."

The ruddy glow of the casinos lit the sky and trees like a stationary forest fire. But gradually this fell behind them, and the lights that shone along the lakeshore were fewer and more furtive. Occasionally Jason grumbled that at night it was hard to tell one cove from another. But in any case, he said, they still had a ways to go.

Once Aryl stopped to pull her boots back on, but that didn't help much against the numbing cold or the little trough of icy water that kept sloshing back and forth in the bottom of the canoe. The world seemed to be composed of cold and dark and the hypnotic swing and dip of the paddles.

Slowly, slowly, Aryl began to see a change in the sky, or at least something seemed to be getting dimmer—either her eyes or the strange star patterns overhead. In the east, the velvet black looked a little faded. "Is dawn coming, do you think?" she said at last.

Jason's voice behind her sounded as if he'd just awakened, though his paddle had never stopped. "Yes, I think it is. And we don't have much farther to go. Let's move closer into shore."

With a few smooth backstrokes, he sent them angling inward to where the pines now showed as a dark fringe against a slightly lighter sky.

In the west the moon was almost touching the dark chain of mountains. Its light had changed from a bright, clear silver to a mellow gold, and by it Aryl suddenly saw a shape humping out of the dark water ahead.

"There's something in the way!"

Jason dug his paddle into frantic backstrokes. "Rocks! Paddle on the other side!"

The hulking shape skimmed by on the right side with only one quiver of contact.

"Rocks creep way out into the water around those points," Jason said in a slightly shaky voice. "This cove isn't the right one, the trees come too close to the water's edge. But I think the next one might be it."

When, at a more cautious distance, they rounded the next point, Aryl thought this cove looked much like the others. But the ghostly moonlight did show trees shrinking back from the shore, exposing flat land that stretched some distance back. Jason brought them in close enough to hear the steady rasping slap of waves against sand.

"Let's pull in here," Jason said at last. "I'm pretty sure it's the right cove. But we may have overshot it in the dark, so I don't want to go any farther." With a few strokes he turned the prow toward the pale curve of beach. "Now paddle hard!"

Muscles protesting, Aryl redoubled her efforts. The boat knifed toward the shore, then, after a grating thump, slid far up onto the sand.

"Now hop out," Jason ordered, "and pull it up a little farther."

Numbly Aryl stepped over the side and stumbled onto the suddenly steady ground. She grabbed at the wooden gunwale and tugged the canoe up another couple of feet. Then, slumping to the cool sand in an exhausted heap, she completely ignored Jason's suggestion, when he'd joined her on the beach, that they pull the boat still farther above the waterline.

"Well, all right, we'll leave it," he conceded, plopping down beside her with the wicker hamper. "Let's eat some of these sandwiches while we wait for it to get light enough to see where we are."

Soon, through an energy-reviving jam sandwich, Aryl said, "Those two certainly were interesting."

Jason chuckled. "The Bentson sisters? Yeah. Most human beings don't have quite their ability for taking things in stride."

"I suppose if one has an unusual enough mind, nothing outside can appear too unusual."

"No amount of craziness can outcrazy them, you mean?"

"Well, perhaps—"

"Hush! Do you hear that?"

"I don't hear anything."

"That's what I mean. A second ago that whole swamp back there was chirping with frogs. They've all stopped."

Aryl strained her ears and realized that the silence was vibrating. Like a subtle pain it slowly formed into a familiar throbbing sound.

Together they shifted around and looked over the dark, shapeless swamp. One, then another, glowing red ring rose above the distant trees and shot into the graying sky.

As the ships sped over head, Aryl flattened herself into the cold, gritty sand. Then numbly she rolled over and watched the red specks retreat and vanish. After all this effort, it was over. They had arrived too late.

fifteen

THE SKY AND LAKE WERE FLAT AND GRAY WITH MORNING. Fish were jumping after low-skimming insects, sending widening circles over the mirror-calm water. But Jason didn't notice. He was aware only of the emptiness inside him, and of one surprising irrelevant fact: Tsorians cry when they are unhappy. He wondered if Aryl was surprised to have learned the same thing about humans.

She was curled up on the sand, but he was afraid to do the same, almost as if his heaviness would turn him into stone. Though that might be better. He forced his mind away from the pain toward petty details.

Where would they go now? Back to the Bentson sisters, of course, at least to return the canoe, but they could hardly stay there. For all he knew, there was nothing left of the Bay Area. His Uncle Carl, his father's brother, had not, it seemed, been at the cabin. So maybe he could go to his place in Red Bluff.

But what about Aryl? She might be the only Tsorian left on Earth. And Earth wouldn't be a healthy place for her, not with the Hykzoi in charge. It probably wouldn't be very healthy for any of them.

Suddenly Aryl jerked upright. "Jason," she said in a

low, tense voice, "When that old lady described the Hyk-zoi attack on the cabin, what did she say about the ship leaving?"

"Huh? I don't remember exactly. She said it looked like a red belt buckle, and then there was talk about the color of the weapon beams. Then she said that once the captives were hauled aboard, they took off."

"Yes, but it didn't fly away alone, did it?"

"No, there was another ship, I think. Or was it two?"

"I seem to remember two."

"So?"

"So, if there were three ships in all, three ships might have landed at those condominiums. But we only saw two take off."

His chest tightened with so much hope it frightened him. "But another could have taken off earlier."

"It could have, right away or while we were sleeping, but once we were on the lake, under that great empty sky, we would surely have seen it."

Jason jumped up so suddenly that a gull foraging on the beach took off with an indignant squawk. "Then they could both still be prisoners back there!"

"It's possible there's still a battle going on, and all spare Hykzoi ships were called in. But one ship might have been left to guard the prisoners. After all, the natives don't look like much of a threat."

"Well, here's one native who plans to be. Let's go!"

Aryl joined him as Jason forged off eastward.

Behind the beach, the sand was dotted with gray-green sage, which gave way to feeble-looking willows and then to rustling grass. Tall green blades rose from dry brown ones, meshing together into a springy, crackling carpet. Occasionally their steps brought an upwelling of brown water or loosed a startled volley of insects or tiny green frogs.

They headed east toward a shoulder of mountain, still dark against the backdrop of a nearly risen sun. Pines flowed down the mountain's steep slope and then westward toward the lake. Where the trees met the marshy meadows, there stood a crescent of modern-looking buildings, windows gleaming dully in the predawn light.

Their route took them over a grassy hummock, and from there they could see to the base of the distant buildings. Squatting on a patch of unnaturally lush greenery was the dull red of a Hykzoi ship. The two looked at each other and grinned.

Suddenly Aryl's expression changed to alarm. She shot out a clawed hand, flattening Jason beside her onto the brittle grass. "If we can see them, they can see us. They could be watching from the windows of that building."

Jason splayed himself so low to the ground he felt like one of those run-over frogs. "Then let's get over to those trees and work our way back through the woods. They don't have X-ray vision, do they?"

"Not that I know of."

Crawling back down, they crouched low beneath the quavering reeds and scuttled toward the dark spur of pine trees that jutted lakeward. Jason noticed that Aryl flinched at the occasional bird or striped water snake that hurried out of her way, but she kept quiet. They had quit trying to keep to the drier grounds, and their feet, squelching into brown water, stirred up a stench of rot and decay.

The sun broke clear of the mountain just as they reached the sheltering band of trees. With relief they both straightened up and leaned against the rough bark of the pines.

Suddenly Aryl pulled her hand away and said, "What is this stuff?"

Sunlight glowed innocently on the amber drops smeared all over her hand. Jason grinned maliciously. "It's pitch. Smells nice, doesn't it?"

"Nasty sticky stuff! How do I get it off?"

"Rub it in the dirt, that'll make it less sticky. Now, let's move. Stay several trees deep into the woods and keep an eye on those buildings."

They hurried as quietly as they could over the forest floor, but it seemed to be booby-trapped with cracking twigs and pinecones to stumble over. To make matters worse, a couple of crows took loud, cawing exception to their intrusion. Jason just hoped these Hykzoi were not attentive woodsmen.

At last they were as close to the buildings as the trees would take them. Crouching down, they peered through the leaves of a low, scraggly bush.

Two many-windowed buildings rose seven stories into the air, curving protectively around a carpet of closely cropped green. Near one edge crouched the Hykzoi ship. From this angle, Jason could clearly see what appeared to be the body of the ship, the thick rectangular bar that hung below the thin, more fragile-looking ring. He glanced at Aryl, but her attention seemed focused on the grass.

"Why is the ground so different there?"

"Uh? Oh, it's a putting green. They grow it that way to play golf, a dumb game where people swat at balls with sticks."

"Doesn't sound any dumber than a lot of the games my father's described from around the universe." The thought seemed to send her mind off on another track. "Those ships taking off may be a good sign. This war might not be over yet."

So who cares about your stupid wars, Jason thought with automatic scorn. But suddenly he realized his reaction didn't spring from real feeling anymore. Maybe he did care about their wars—a little. He frowned. "Do you think they're holding the captives in the ship or the buildings?"

"The buildings probably. That's why they landed here, I guess. Those strikeships aren't very roomy. The crew has probably moved in temporarily as well. I don't see anyone about."

Jason would as soon he never did. The Bentson sisters' description of these new aliens made him distinctly uneasy. "There're no windows on the narrow ends of the buildings. We can sneak up to them that way."

Getting down nearly on all fours, they darted behind sagebrush until this gave way to ornamental shrubs. Jason tried not to look at his companion. In this stance, her differently articulated limbs made her appear startlingly alien again.

Any second he expected to hear a Hykzoi guard call out, though what a Hykzoi warning call sounded like, he couldn't guess. Maybe they didn't warn. Maybe they just zapped first and asked questions later. If it weren't his mom in there . . .

Finally, they were leaning up against the blind end of the building. "Couldn't they be in the other building as easily as this one?" Jason said, trying to calm his breathing.

"Maybe, but their ship's parked closer to this one. And anyway, didn't you notice something funny about some of the windows?"

"No."

"On this building, one whole floor looked kind of

blanked out like something was stretched over the windows. The fifth floor up, I think."

"So what does that mean?"

"I don't know. You're the native here. That's unusual, though, isn't it?"

"Yeah, I guess. So we've just got to sneak into a building that could be crawling with Hykzoi and take a squint at the fifth floor. Simple."

The first part did prove simple. At their end, an unlocked door led into the basement. A single bare lightbulb lit a large space filled with the odor of cleaning supplies and rot.

"Whew," Jason said. "Smells like no one dared pick up the garbage today."

At the sound of his voice, there was a raspy shuffling at the far end of the room. Something was working at what was apparently an open fuse box. It turned and Jason recognized it immediately. A huge, animated Swiss army knife. Its body was flat and elongated, and various-shaped appendages were moving in and out of slots in its side.

"Down!" Aryl squeaked as one appendage raised toward them. Jason dove for the concrete floor. The air above him crackled and fizzed.

Beside him, he glimpsed Aryl dart away as the lawn mower she'd been crouching behind twisted in a beam of deepest red.

In panic, Jason rolled behind a jutting piece of wall. Another red beam clipped off a chink above him, but most of the sizzling attack was focused elsewhere. The creature seemed to be after the Tsorian threat, not the inconsequential native.

Jason peered around the corner. Still standing by the fuse box, the Hykzoi had turned its flat body sideways as it followed Aryl's flight. Obviously whatever it used for eyes were traveling that way too. An appendage shot out another scarlet beam, and under cover of the crackling sound, Jason slipped out of hiding and looked frantically for some weapon. Grabbing a large rake from against the wall, he rushed at the creature.

The Hykzoi flipped around and aimed at Jason just as the metal prongs of the rake smashed into its middle. Flailing, the thing staggered back, one pronged appendage jabbing into the fuse box.

Suddenly the whole alien arced and crackled with electricity. The room's single light bulb blinked out, and Jason finally heard what a Hykzoi sounded like. A high grating cry sawed through his skull. It must have alerted the entire world.

✖ s i x t e e n ✖

WHEN THE SCREAM HAD DIED, ARYL SLOWLY GOT UP FROM behind the crates where she'd huddled. One side of her leg was singed raw, but fear overwhelmed the pain. Cautiously she peered out into the large silent room.

To her astonishment, Jason was alive and standing. At his feet sprawled the crumpled, charred body of the Hykzoi. Jason turned toward her, his stunned look changing to one of relief. "Oh. It didn't fry you."

"Not from want of trying. You really killed it?"

"Well, it sort of did that itself."

She looked at the rake still clutched in Jason's hand. "Not voluntarily, I suspect. What'll we do with it?"

"We could haul it into a broom closet," he said, his lip curling. Obviously he felt about that dead charred thing the same way she did.

"No, let's leave it. If anyone comes to investigate, they'll think it just electrocuted itself accidentally."

"Good, then let's split! There ought to be stairs somewhere."

Aryl wasn't sure that the scream had been loud enough to summon help, but she didn't want to stick around to see. Anxiously she followed Jason as, after several false turns, he lead them to the base of a concrete and metal staircase.

"Definitely not the posh route for the rich tenants," he commented, "but it'll get us up."

As they passed the door for the second floor, they heard faint grating chirps and whistles from the other side.

"Hykzoi," Aryl whispered, and they practically flew up the next three flights. Finally, heart pounding and out of breath, she slumped down beside Jason, just outside the door marked FIVE.

But immediately her relief vanished. Frowning, she got up and examined the edge of the door. It seemed to be covered with some sort of gray, gummy material. Gingerly she poked at it. It felt hard and slick. Her claws couldn't begin to pry it away.

"Weird stuff," Jason said as he joined her. "But I guess it shows that they're in there, all right."

"This must have been what I saw on the windows. They've got the whole floor sealed. Saves the bother of guarding prisoners, I guess."

Jason frowned. "Yeah, and it shoots my idea of lowering ourselves from a window on the floor above."

"Maybe we could find some sort of tool in the basement that'd cut through this stuff," Aryl suggested.

"Garbage!"

Aryl scowled. She hadn't thought her idea was that bad.

Jason grinned. "I bet the Hykzoi don't know about garbage chutes."

"About what?"

"See? You don't either. They've got them in posh places like this. Shafts in the central hallways where you can dump your garbage so you don't have to haul it downstairs. They connect every floor!"

Slowly Aryl smiled as the picture fell into place. "So if we go up to the next floor . . ."

"Right!" Jason was already on his way.

He was waiting by the door, watching as she limped up the last few steps. "Hey, you didn't tell me you were badly hurt."

"That's because I'm not," she snapped, trying not to cringe as movement pulled at the seared skin on her leg. "Let's get on with it."

Shrugging, Jason cautiously opened the door. Peering over his shoulder, Aryl thought the hallway not only looked empty, it felt empty. She followed him inside. The carpet, thick and springy under her boots, had a nauseating pattern in purple and pink.

The muffled sound of their footsteps only accentuated the utter silence around them. Doors ranged symmetrically on either side of the hall. Most were closed, but some had been left gaping open. Aryl hoped they wouldn't stumble across the charred remains of residents who hadn't made it out in time.

"Ah-ha!" Jason whispered, and Aryl flinched. He was looking at a large metal flap set into the wall of the hallway and painted the same pinkish color. Pushing it open, he looked down. Even from where she stood, Aryl caught the wiff of garbage.

"Whew!" Jason said. "Guess that's what we want, all right."

"And we're supposed to just crawl down it?"

"I don't know about you, but I'll need a rope. Maybe I can find what we need in one of these apartments. Obviously not everyone stopped to lock up."

He disappeared through one of the open doors, returning a few minutes later with an assortment of cords clearly meant for purposes other than climbing. Soon, however, they'd tied them together into a fifteen-foot length. Then, dragging a gilded table from one apartment, they placed it in front of the shaft and tied one end of the cord around a leg.

"I hope this antique is up to this," Jason said doubtfully as he climbed on top. The table creaked but stayed in one piece.

He dropped the rest of the cord down the shaft. "When I'm safe on the next floor, I'll give the rope a couple of tugs and you follow me. You're not claustrophobic, are you?"

"What's that?"

"Afraid of tight places."

"Of course not," she snorted, glad that Tsorian complexions didn't betray emotions as easily as some human complexions seemed to.

"Good." He lifted the flap, stuck one foot in while holding the metal frame, then awkwardly swung in the other leg. Grabbing the rope, he started lowering himself down. Aryl held the metal flap to keep it from clanging shut, then lowered it gently on the taut, occasionally twitching rope.

Aryl definitely did not want to go down there. Yet somehow standing alone in this abandoned native dwelling seemed almost worse. Almost. There was no question about it: Tsorians did not like tight, enclosed places. That's why so many of their walls, even on board ship, were transparent. Still, if her father was down there . . .

The table jerked as the rope tugged twice. Before panic could immobilize her, Aryl crawled onto the table and wriggled her legs into the metal shaft. She grabbed the rope and for an awful moment thought that she'd stick half in and half out. Then she twisted around to a better angle and lowered herself down. The stench of rotting meat and vegetation wafted up, nearly choking her. She forced herself to lower her body into it.

With a clang the metal flap shut her into the tight, foul darkness. Somehow she kept herself from scrambling back up. Escape was there below her too, she told herself desperately. All she had to do was climb down to it.

One hand fumbling past the other, she moved down and down. All sides of the cold metal shaft were slick with rot. They pressed in as if they wanted to crush her. She could feel the weight of the building focusing in on this one spot.

She had to find the way out! Frantically in the total darkness, her feet groped along the confining walls. They all felt the same. Had she passed the exit already? No, it might seem as if she'd been in here forever, but probably she hadn't moved very far. Lowering herself farther, she concentrated on the exit. At last, her boots tapped against a different type of metal. A few more feet, and she could see a thin square outline of light. With one hand she pushed open the flap. Then, letting go of the rope, she hoisted herself out, hardly caring whether she tumbled onto a rug or a whole nest of Hykzoi.

When she sat up, blinking, her panic had seeped away. She was alone again in a hallway similar to the one above. Except she could hear subdued voices coming from a room at the far end. Human voices, and Jason's was among them. She sprinted down the corridor and careened into the room.

It was strangely dark. The electricity was out, and the gray seal over the windows was only slightly transparent. Still, she could see several figures. One was a native male with no hair on his head, and nearby, Jason was standing with arms around his mother. A Tsorian was lying on a couch. His eyes were open, and he was talking with the others.

She ran to him, then remembering propriety, skidded into an awkward salute.

"Aryl!" Rogav said hoarsely, and smiled. Forgetting everything, she dropped down beside him and fell against his chest, relishing his strong, gentle hug.

"I didn't really think any Hykzoi could break this bonding," he said softly. "But maybe you'd better not crush me, now that I'm just getting my body to function again."

Flustered, she helped him sit up, then noticed how wet his head and shoulders seemed to be. Marilyn, standing above them, laughed and put down the bowl and cloth she'd been holding.

"I've been daubing gallons of ice water over him, but he seems to be fully back with us now. I think the Hykzoi upped their beam on him a little. The professor and I came around a lot sooner."

For the first time Aryl really focused on the bald human, presumably "the professor," standing behind the couch. She nodded at him, then looked back at her father, noticing the half-healed scar across his forehead and cheek. "Father, are you all right? Are you hurt?"

"Well, the Hykzoi have left me feeling like an imploded star, but otherwise I'm fine."

"But . . ."

"That," he said, gingerly touching the scar, "is ancient history." Briefly he looked at Marilyn and smiled. "We've all been through a lot together, and for the moment it's left us firmly on the same side."

"I hate to break up this multiple reunion," Professor Ackerman said, "but maybe we ought to get out of here."

"Agreed," Rogav answered, command slipping easily

into his voice, "but there are some things I need to know first. You and Jason go gather some more ropes for his ingenious escape hatch."

The two hurried off, joined after a moment by Marilyn. Aryl sat beside her father on the couch.

"We followed events on the radio in the cabin," Rogav said. "But those were native reporters. What's your assessment? Are we two the only Tsorians left on the planet?"

"Possibly. It sounds as if most of our minor planetary posts are gone. Certainly the Headquarters is, though I think most of the personnel had left by then and certainly most of the ships had. The body of the fleet was planning to deploy near Mars, so if any holdings were defended, that base would have been."

"Ah. And you've no idea how they fared?"

"No, I don't. But enough of our fleet must remain to be giving the Hykzoi some sort of resistance. If they'd had a clear victory, they probably wouldn't have bothered to keep you around."

"Exactly what I was thinking. Definitely the professor's right, we ought to get going."

"I'd better warn you," she whispered. "You're not going to like the way out."

"Is it worse than staying with the Hykzoi?"

"Not quite."

"Then show me to it."

With Aryl's help, Rogav got unsteadily to his feet and began walking around, trying to work the paralysis out of his legs.

Professor Ackerman returned, beaming. "We're in luck. The former denizens of this place seem to have been water-skiers. There was some good strong nylon rope in the closet. We eked it out with other stuff, but it ought to hold."

They were just at the apartment door when a gargled hooting rose from outside. "What's that?" Marilyn and the professor said together.

"Sounds Hykzoi," Rogav commented.

Aryl nodded while trying to hurry the others along. "They've probably just found the fellow downstairs. Jason killed him." She was slightly surprised at the tone of pride in her voice.

"It was more of an accident really," Jason said, an unmistakable blush creeping over his face. "We ran into him in the basement where I think he was trying to patch up the electricity. He started shooting, at Aryl mainly, and I kind of pushed him into the fuse box. Electrocuted."

Marilyn stopped dead in the hall and hugged her son. "Good night, Jason, I've gotten you into the most ghastly things."

"Hey, Mom, you didn't get me into them. *I* got me into them. And right now, I think we all ought to get out of them."

They hurried down the long hall to the garbage chute where Professor Ackerman tied one end of the rope to a sturdy metal vacuum cleaner wand and jammed it across the chute's mouth. The howling wails outside were now rising from several voices.

"Ritual shock and mourning," Rogav interpreted. "Usually preparatory to vengeance. We're all right as long as they don't connect that death with us."

"And if they do?" Marilyn asked.

"Then we have a very few minutes to live."

✖ s e v e n t e e n ✖

JASON CLOSED THE FLAP DOWN ON THE ROPE, GETTING A last glimpse of Aryl's pale hair disappearing like smoke into the darkness. He suspected she was a tad more claustrophobic than she'd admitted. Not that he was looking forward to this trip himself, but it beat standing there waiting for the Hykzoi to suddenly burst in.

Professor Ackerman had gone down first to see if all was clear. He'd been followed by Jason's mother and then by Rogav. Aryl and Jason had a major squabble over who should be next, but finally he'd persuaded her to follow her father. Now, impatiently, he awaited his turn. If only these places had multiple garbage chutes the way Tsorians had banks of lift tubes.

The wailing had died down outside. He wondered what sort of weird death rituals these things engaged in. Maybe they liked to immolate bystanders on the deceased's funeral pyre. Maybe they'd come bursting up here any second demanding a life for a life. Maybe first, though, they'd practice dreadful tortures on him. They probably had various ghastly appendages specialized for that sort of thing.

He yelped when the rope jerked and went slack. In an instant he grabbed it and wormed his way into the chute.

He was well on his way down before he remembered how much he hated this. Still it was lots better than waiting to be dismembered by an animated jackknife.

After a seemingly endless descent, his feet clumped against a slant in the chute. He must have reached bottom. He was just fumbling for the flap when he heard noises in the room outside. Like chickens clucking from the bottom of a well. Hykzoi talking.

Jason shuddered and clung tighter to the rope. Had they captured the others? He didn't hear any human or Tsorian voices. Maybe they'd just come back to view the scene of the "accident."

For minutes, Jason half hung, half crouched in the cramped, smelly darkness. Then the sounds faded away. Cautiously he lifted the metal flap and, crouching down, peered out. In the dim light, the basement was empty and silent. The charred wreck by the fuse box had been removed.

He stepped out into a bin of garbage. Cursing, he extricated himself, then began tiptoeing toward the door. Where could the others have gone? They hadn't planned this part.

Suddenly something snaked out from the wall, grabbed him around the mouth, and pulled him into a utility closet crammed with warm, anxious bodies, human and Tsorian.

"Can you still hear them?" the professor whispered in his ear.

"Just a distant babble," Jason said with incredible relief.

Behind him, Rogav's rough Tsorian voice whispered, "Then they won't be all the way to the front yet. We'd better wait until they are."

For several minutes the five of them waited in the tiny closet. Giddily Jason wondered if they were breaking some sort of Guinness world record: largest number of humans and Tsorians in a single closet.

When the voices finally faded, the five unpacked themselves from each other and headed cautiously for the outside door. The professor slipped out, then motioned for the others to follow. Crouching low, they scuttled across an empty stretch of lawn toward a screen of trees.

Jason expected to be blown to cinders any second, but at last they were all huddled at a spot where a giant tree had fallen over, raising roots and dirt as a welcome shield against the occupied building behind them.

"Well, where now?" Marilyn said between puffs for breath.

"Stateline's not far from here, is it?" the professor asked.

Jason nodded in reply, pointing vaguely south through the trees. "Four or five miles that way."

"Okay," Marilyn said. "But if we go to Stateline, then what? There'd be transportation and communications and such, but I suspect some of us wouldn't get a very good reception. And if those Hykzoi find us gone, that's probably the first place they'll think of searching—or burning. I think we'd be better off away from any settlements."

"Marilyn's right," Rogav said, running a hand over his haggard face. "But only for you three. I have to try to get in touch with my fleet, if there's anything left of it. Possibly I could use some sort of native radio device, but I don't know if I could find one strong enough. The only communicator I can count on to do that is in that Hykzoi ship, which means we're going to have to sneak aboard it. But you three had better clear out. This is our war, after all, even if you are the victims."

148

Jason felt an unexpected wrench inside. He glanced at Aryl, but she was looking down at a patch of dirt.

Marilyn cleared her throat. "Rogav, there you go again being all dictatorial. This may have started out as your war, but the choice of battlefields has made it ours too. You'll have a hard time capturing that ship with only two of you."

Before the Tsorian commander could reply, the professor added, "It's like I've been telling him for these last few weeks. The problem with imperialists is that they never let their wards make their own decisions. Like a bunch of overprotective parents. You agree, Jason?"

With astonishment, Jason looked at these two "Resisters." Those weeks in the cabin had clearly changed their personal attitudes toward their captive, and apparently these last few days had altered some of their political views as well. But then, he didn't exactly feel untouched himself. He nodded. "Sure. I wouldn't want to miss the last thrilling episode."

Aryl grinned at him.

"Well, then," Rogav said, not looking the least displeased, "we need a plan. Aryl, were there any guards on that ship when you came?"

"Not that I saw."

"I didn't see any either," Jason said. "But it's parked pretty close to the building. Maybe they consider that security enough."

"Yes, that's the problem," Rogav said, lapsing into thought.

"Obviously we need to draw their attention somewhere else for a bit," the professor suggested. "You know, create a diversion."

"That, Professor, is probably the oldest tactic in the

universe. Of course, the reason it's still around is that it keeps working. What do you suggest?"

"The three of us attack from the far side while you two run for the ship."

"Attack with what?" Jason asked. "Rocks and pinecones?"

"How about blowing something up?" Marilyn suggested.

"You could blow up those automobiles," Aryl said, pointing to the parking lot. "That one of yours, Jason, blew up splendidly."

Jason's mother shot him a look but didn't say anything.

The professor nodded. "Yes, matches in the gas tank."

"That would blow us up too," Jason objected.

"Couldn't we put in some sort of fuse?" his mother asked.

The professor slapped his hands together. "That's it, then. We three sneak over to the parking lot, stick strips torn from our clothing into some gas tanks, light them, and run like hell for the trees."

"While Aryl and I run for the ship," Rogav added. "You ought to have been a soldier, Professor."

"Up until recently, I preferred theorizing to acting." Ackerman stood up. "Well, let's deploy."

Cautiously the five crept back toward the outer fringe of trees. For a moment, Rogav and Marilyn stepped aside and spoke quietly to each other. Jason looked at Aryl, noticing suddenly how the clear mountain light made her hair glow like mist. He slowly turned red and tried to force out the right words. "Aryl, I'm sorry about . . . everything. Well, almost everything, I guess. Now that I've gotten to know you, I mean."

To Jason's surprise, Aryl, always glib of tongue, seemed

to be having as much difficulty as he. "I'm the one who should be apologizing, for a lot of things. I guess I should be thanking you too."

"Come on, everyone, no time for teary farewells," the professor said. "Though I've got to admit, I'll miss all those late-night discussions of Tsorian astrophysics. It helped make up for ten years of academic frustration." He started toward the parking lot, then looked back. "Good luck, you purple imperialists."

Jason's sight seemed oddly blurred as he began running behind the first rank of trees. But gradually fear took over. He felt that every dark window in those buildings was concealing an armed Hykzoi staring at him. Yet no beams of red light shot out. He could hear his mother running less than silently just behind him.

Out of breath, the three humans finally reached the spot where the asphalt parking lot came closest to the encircling trees. They were still about a hundred feet of scrubby grassland away, however. Peering out, Jason could see several Hykzoi moving in and out of the building's lobby. He couldn't tell what they were doing. Hopefully they didn't have enough compassion for their prisoners to bring them food or check on how they were.

At the far end of the putting green, the Hykzoi ship waited innocently. Jason could see that something was dangling down from the thick, shoeboxlike crossbar. It might be a rope ladder if it weren't so oddly arranged. He didn't see anything else, though. No sneaking movement of maroon and black shapes. Good. Maybe if he couldn't see them, the Hykzoi couldn't either.

Jason jumped as the professor touched his shoulder. He'd taken off his shirt and torn it into shreds. Ceremoniously he handed several to Jason and to his mother along

151

with a packet of matches each. "Knew there was a good reason for not giving up smoking," he whispered. Then, getting on all fours, he began skittering across the grass toward the nearest of the parked cars.

Jason looked at his matchbook: "Starlight Mortuary, a Future of Eternal Peace." Great. He dropped it into his pocket. His mother turned to him and gave him a quick, teary hug. Then she walked west a ways through the trees and finally crept across the open space to the far end of the parking lot. Sighing, Jason crouched down into the tall, prickly grass and headed for a spot midway between the other two.

The scrubby stretch ended at a feeble bank of ornamental shrubbery. Jason squinted through the leaves, and seeing that the other two had already moved in, he scuttled like a crab across the asphalt.

The first car he tried had a firmly locked gas cap. So did the second. But the third twisted off easily. Just then a very poor imitation of an owl call floated over the parking lot. One of the saboteurs was ready. Jason hoped the Hykzoi didn't know anything about native birds. He looked at the strips of cloth in his hand, doubled one over, then stuck it into the mouth of the gas tank. Good thing Ackerman had decided to tear up his own shirt, Jason thought, since the particular T-shirt he was wearing had his favorite rock group on it.

Nervously pulling the matchbook from his pocket, he made his own owl call. Sure were a lot of owls about in broad daylight. A minute later a third call rose from another part of the parking lot. The two Tsorians had better be ready, because here comes the diversion, he thought grimly.

Shakily Jason struck a match. It failed. He lit another

and applied the wavering flame to the cloth. Nothing happened, and the match sputtered out. He tried again. Was the blasted material flame-retardant or something? He tried yet again, and this time it caught, smoldering at one end of the cloth in a feeble worm of flame. Then with a sudden whoosh, the cloth flared up.

In a panic Jason leaped back and began running for the trees. At one end of the parking lot there was a swoosh; then a loud explosion. He looked back and saw the professor running like a madman. Behind Jason, his own car exploded with a deafening roar almost obscuring the third explosion to his right.

Heat smashed him from behind like a fist. He staggered, caught his foot in a hole, and sprawled facedown in the stickery grass. He was elbowing himself up when he saw a dark-red beam slice through the air and catch the professor in midstride. Arms and legs suddenly aflame, the man cartwheeled through the air like some horrible firework. His screams were sharp and short.

With a surprising pang, Aryl watched the three natives slipping away through the trees. This shouldn't hurt, she told herself. These were aliens on an alien world. But somehow that word didn't have quite the same meaning anymore.

She looked at her father and saw that he was also watching the retreating forms. Then he straightened up and with a gesture to her began walking in the opposite direction. Aryl followed, trying to keep up and walk quietly at the same time, but the ground seemed littered with all manner of things that cracked.

Finally they worked their way around to where the short-cropped patch of grass came closest to the trees. Not far from its edge sat the Hykzoi ship. Aryl shuddered, fascinated and horrified. She'd never seen one this close. And now she had to do more than look at it, she had to get into it.

Following Rogav's lead, Aryl crouched behind a bush and prepared to wait. The dusty-green leaves smelled sharp and medicinal in the late-morning sun. Through the screen they created, she studied the ship and the strange tangled cords that hung from it.

"What's that?" she whispered.

"That's the Hykzoi equivalent of an entry ramp. It fits their odd assortment of legs."

Almost as if on cue, the kinked and twisted cords began to jiggle, and a multilegged Hykzoi scrambled down to the ground. From there it scuttled off toward the building.

"What was it doing there?" Aryl wondered.

"Could be anything. Making repairs, using the communicator, even using the sanitary facilities for all I know. But it better not come back before our friends start their diversion. I feel awfully vulnerable without any weapon."

Aryl looked about, then slipped from her hiding place into the trees. In moments she'd returned with two fallen branches. "How about clubs?"

Rogav chuckled. "Nothing like going native."

"Come on, things here aren't as primitive as all that."

Her father nodded. "I know, Daughter. But they may well be pushed back to that state if we don't succeed in this. So hand over my redoubtable weapon."

For ages, it seemed, they crouched behind the bush. The sun, the exotic smells, the droning insects, had almost lulled Aryl to sleep when a loud explosion tore the air at the far side of the buildings.

She and Rogav tensed as a second and then a third

explosion followed, and Hykzoi burst from the building and started running in that direction.

Like missiles, the two Tsorians darted toward the waiting ship. Everywhere there was noise and frenzy. Several adjacent cars seemed to have blown up as well, and Aryl saw a red energy beam slash through the air. A flaming body spiraled upward. Instantly she felt ill. Jason was agile and quick, but . . .

Rogav, several strides ahead of her, reached the dangling cords and began pulling himself up—just as a Hykzoi appeared at the top and began scrambling down. In startled confusion, they met halfway. Rogav tried to grab the other's slicing limbs as it struggled to bring out and aim its weapon.

For a moment, the climbing frame rocked violently, sounds of the conflict obscured by the noise elsewhere. Then with a sudden jerk, the Hykzoi somersaulted to the ground, landed upright, and aimed its weapon. Aryl leaped forward and brought down her club. Pieces of wood splintered away as the Hykzoi staggered and clattered to the ground.

"Hail primitivism!" Rogav called. "Hurry!"

Leaping over their fallen opponent, Aryl sprang for the climbing frame, and as it swayed and bucked, she scrambled up its awkwardly spaced rungs into the ship.

Once inside, she remained crouching on the floor staring at the very alien-looking interior. Everything seemed oddly angular, and the yellow-green light made her edgy.

Her father's difficulties with the ship were more practical. "In theory I know how to work their equipment, but I don't want to set off any alarms along with the communicator. See if you can find a way to close that hatch—quietly."

Aryl started looking around for controls when suddenly out of the opening she saw a Hykzoi running toward them. It seemed to notice its fallen comrade; then, increasing its speed, it pulled out a weapon.

"Father, they've seen us! We'd better lift off!"

"We can try."

For a moment nothing happened, except that the Hykzoi was getting closer. Then the air began throbbing with noise, and Aryl could see through the overhead view-panels that the encircling red ring, the propulsion unit, was beginning to glow. Suddenly the deck shuddered and she found herself lying on it with the ship now several hundred feet in the air.

Below she could see the burning cars and two natives galloping over open grasslands toward the lake. Running clumsily after them, a couple of Hykzoi were having difficulty aiming their weapons, but the air was still crisscrossed with their beams.

"We've got to help them!" Aryl insisted. Her father, frowning out through a view screen, growled, "The native phrase is 'easier said than done.' "

Before he'd even finished his sentence, however, the twisting of one prismatic dial dropped the ship nearly to the ground. Then they began gliding toward the lake. The pursuit was right before them.

Aryl braced herself and peered out the open hatch. Below were meadow grasses, then suddenly they swept low over two cowering Hykzoi. With a shudder, the ship slowed. The climbing frame, still hanging down, just brushed the tops of bushes.

Suddenly Jason and his mother were below. From where they crouched in the grass, their wide eyes stared up into hers. "Grab the frame!" she yelled over the thrumming of the energy ring. A moment's hesitation, then Jason lunged for the end that was erratically bobbing up and down.

"Keep it steady!" Aryl called over her shoulder.

"Aye, Captain," came her father's dry reply, but the ship did stabilize. In a moment, Marilyn was climbing upward while Jason tried to hold the frame steady for her. When she'd reached the top, he grabbed the lurching cords himself and began following.

Suddenly energy bolts were bursting around him. Some came from the earlier pursuers and some from reinforcements carrying a larger weapon, now aimed directly at the ship.

Vigorously Rogav worked the controls, and the ship shot forward. Below it, the frame swayed wildly. A last energy bolt sliced into a section above and beside Jason, snapping connecting links.

✠ e i g h t e e n ✠

As the air stopped crackling around him, Jason clung fiercely to the remaining rungs. He opened his eyes to see grass whipping by a few feet below him. Beyond stretched the blue of the lake.

In moments they were skimming over the water, the bottom of the climbing frame slapping wildly at the white-capped waves. Jason was afraid to loosen his grip, but was even more afraid that the ship would take another erratic dip. Above the shrieking wind, he could hear voices urging him to climb. Taking his eyes from the inky-blue water, he did. Doggedly he pulled himself up, hand over hand, until other hands grabbed him and pulled him on board.

He rolled over on the metal deck, for a minute too dizzy even to sit up. Then his mother and Aryl helped him onto what was apparently a Hykzoi seat, a shattered-looking prismatic pillar. He leaned against the jagged back and stared out a view screen.

They seemed to be flying over the water like a skipped pebble, less than a dozen feet from the surface. Jason caught a glimpse of an appalled-looking water-skier before they shot over his head. Probably didn't do his form any good, Jason thought, trying to ignore the rapidly approaching far shore with its trees, buildings, and mountains.

Aryl was less reserved, however. "Father, you have noticed those rather high-looking mountains ahead?"

Rogav's only reply was an annoyed grunt, but moments later the ship veered upward. Abruptly Jason slid from the jagged seat. Rolling across the deck, he suddenly found himself staring out the open hatch. His fingers desperately gripped the edge. He had a swirling glimpse of houses and trees before someone hauled him back by his feet.

"Rogav," said his mother's taut voice behind him, "could we please shut this hatch?"

"Perhaps, if you can find the controls."

Avoiding the yawning opening in the middle of the cabin, the three of them set about searching. One control Jason found didn't do anything but dim the lights. Another set off a frantic whirling of vinegar-scented air through the cabin. Finally Aryl discovered a small projection near the hatch itself. Pushing it caused the climbing frame to rattle upward and the hatch to swirl closed like a camera lens. Jason sighed with relief.

Only then did he turn back to the view screen. He was astonished at how high they were, although "height" hardly seemed the right term anymore. Below was a whole relief map of northern California. Directly beneath them, the Sierras were piled up like a crumpled blanket. Then this smoothed into the hazy sweep of the Central Valley and ended in the distant purple of the Coast Ranges. Beyond that, the gray smear of the Pacific Ocean was becoming more visible by the second.

Given the speed at which they were rising, Jason was surprised he didn't feel as if he were on some super elevator—with his stomach left on the ground floor. He wondered how this ship counteracted that.

Beside him, his mother apparently was also noticing the technology. "Poor Professor Ackerman," she said softly. "How he would have loved to see one of these ships on the inside."

Jason nodded but couldn't say anything. The picture of that horrible death was still too vivid. To drive it away, he turned his attention to the control panels.

Aryl had joined her father, and the two Tsorians were puzzling over the unfamiliar controls. Suddenly the sight of them, with his native state rapidly receding in the background, brought the whole thing into focus. Six months ago he'd been down there somewhere, leading a reasonably normal life. Even when he had gotten involved with the Resistance, it had been almost a game. That creature standing there had been the arch-villain, Rogav Jy, the enemy commander. Everything had been clear and impersonal.

And now in a few days the picture had been torn apart and reassembled. The enemy wasn't *the* enemy; the arch-villain was the father of someone he almost considered a friend; the world he'd grown up in had been blown away; he'd just seen a good man give up his life for people he'd tried to defeat; and now he, Jason Sikes, was escaping truly ghastly creatures in a stolen spaceship.

Dizzily he leaned back. But at least there was one fixed point in his life. He had his mother again. Not that she was your average mother, he admitted, but he wouldn't trade all the normality in the world for what they had together. He smiled toward her where she sat on another pillar seat, eyes on the view screen. He didn't totally understand this

160

Tsorian bonding business Aryl kept talking about, but it couldn't be all that different.

At the moment, however, Tsorian father and daughter were looking more worried than sentimental. Rogav turned and frowned at the two humans, adding new shadows to his seamed and craggy face. "I'm afraid we have taken you—what is the native phrase—'from the pot into the oven.'"

"Try 'out of the frying pan into the fire,'" Marilyn suggested.

"Whatever. But you might have been better off if we'd left you running through that swamp dodging blaster fire. Professor Ackerman could be the lucky one. If the Hykzoi back there manage to inform others of our escape, we could be intercepted at any moment."

"Can't you contact your own ships?" Marilyn asked. "If there are any around, that is."

"That's the problem, or one of them. Obviously there's no exclusive Tsorian band on this Hykzoi communication device, and not knowing where our ships might be, I'll have to send a pretty broad spectrum appeal."

"But if you broadcast the coordinates where they can meet us," Marilyn pointed out, "mightn't the Hykzoi pick that up too?"

"Maybe, but I think I know a few codes they haven't broken yet." With a few more adjustments on one set of controls, he leaned forward and launched into harsh, guttural Tsorian, repeating the short message over and over.

Jason had switched his attention back to the view screen when Aryl came up behind him. "Jason, come look at this."

He followed to where a large hexagonal frame was set into the floor. She crouched down, pressed a metal stud in the frame, and suddenly that section of floor turned transparent; another twist and it looked like metal again.

"Not bad!" he said, twisting the stud himself. The land below was green and brown with occasional cloud shadows rolling over it. Roads crisscrossed in seemingly random patterns until they converged in geometric splotches that must be cities.

"Look!" Jason said, pointing to a glint of silver moving through the sky below them. He wondered if the passengers were pointing up at the spaceship.

"Looks like a commercial airliner," his mother commented, coming up behind them.

"I'm surprised," Aryl said, "with all this happening that they're still running flights."

Marilyn shook her head. "I'm not. When you first invaded, we stopped everything. But when the world didn't come to an end, we started up our lives almost as if nothing had changed. We've gotten pretty good at pretending that." She was silent a moment then added, "I used to think that was cowardly." She turned and walked over to join Rogav.

For a moment, Jason watched them. The Tsorian was huddled intently over the console while the human stood behind him, a hand casually on his shoulder.

Jason turned back to the view below him, but he kept thinking about his mother's last sentence. Maybe it was *not* adapting to reality that was cowardly. He needed to think about that; he needed to think about a lot of things.

But there wasn't time now. Rogav interrupted his steady broadcast with a sharp exclamation Jason recognized as a Tsorian curse. The Commander grabbed the controls and abruptly the ship jolted into a violent turn, then an evasive swoop to the north. Jason found himself lying facedown in the middle of the viewport, the landscape lurching sickeningly below him. With a whimper he reached up and twisted the stud.

"Whew!" He rolled over on the now solid-seeming floor. "What happened?"

"That!" Aryl said, sitting up and pointing out the front view screen.

Two glowing red rings were bearing down on them from above. A burst of squealing language blared from the communicator, followed in moments by a red flare from one of the ships. Rogav was now working the controls intently. The ship half flipped over and then shot sideways. An energy burst passed them in a glittering shimmer. Then the ship shuddered as Rogav got off an attack of his own.

Their attackers launched a new volley as Rogav sent the ship rocketing upward while firing several more shots. One of the red ships suddenly blossomed into flame. Flaring bits shot off like fireworks, then the whole fireball plummeted downward.

Aryl, Jason, and his mother let out a cheer. Jauntily, Rogav saluted them, then turned back to the screen.

Their elation was short-lived. The remaining ship launched a new attack, which, despite their stomach-wrenching evasions, filled the view screens with spinning red sparks. The next shot hit them.

For a moment the world was soundless and blindingly red. Then it exploded with sound. Jason was flung against some metal surface. They were tumbling so much he couldn't tell if it was a floor, ceiling, or wall.

Slowly, like a fever, the red glow and the sound faded. Jason opened his eyes. The violent twisting had subsided into a lazy spiral; the ship was more or less upright.

Amazed that he could, Jason sat up. His mother and

Rogav were sprawled over the controls like a couple of rag dolls. The air at that end of the cabin was fuzzy with a violet haze. He smelled a thick sweet odor vaguely like licorice. Dizzily he stood up.

"Don't! Stay away from there!" Aryl croaked in a weak voice. She staggered to her feet beside him. "That's althon gas—the coils must have ruptured."

"Will it kill them?"

"It could, and us too. Where's that air clearer?"

For a moment, Jason's mind was a blank. The smell of licorice was getting worse. Feeling weak and dizzy, he staggered over to a control knob he thought he had tried earlier. Was this the one, or would it blow up the ship? Didn't much matter. He pressed it and hung on to the wall, wondering if he would throw up or pass out first.

Slowly he realized that there was air whipping about him as if he were standing on a sailboat. The cabin now smelled more of pickles than licorice. The combination didn't do his stomach any good, but his head was clearing.

Unsteadily he walked toward the controls. Aryl was already there, gently turning her father over. The old scar on his forehead was now supplemented by a large bruise, showing midnight blue against the maroon of his skin.

"Let's lay them down on the deck," she said. "If the althon gas were going to kill them, it would have done it already. So they should be all right once they come out of this. Good thing our deflectors held as long as they did, or we'd all be cinders by now."

Jason hoisted up his mother and moved her to the floor, trying to make her as comfortable as possible. That gas leak hadn't been the only damage. One side of her face was singed, and smoke was rising from some of the controls.

Standing up again, Jason saw Aryl gazing fearfully

through the upper view screen. The red ring hung way above them now.

"I don't think the controls are totally shot," she said. "But if I try fiddling with them and this ship shows any signs of life, they'll be after us in a moment."

"And these deflector things are out of commission?"

"We couldn't withstand someone throwing rocks at us."

For a while they stood in silence, but the ship's steady downward spiral was making Jason dizzy again. He leaned against a pillar seat and closed his eyes. "If we keep going down like this," he ventured at last, "we'll smash up in somebody's pasture."

"And if I fiddle with the controls too soon, we'll be blown apart first."

"Well, just don't wait too long." Jason crouched miserably on the deck. Perversely he reached across and flicked the view screen to clear again. It wasn't really pastures they'd smash into, he realized. It was a city, or at least some sort of suburban sprawl. Roads, housing developments, shopping malls, all were spinning closer and closer toward him. "Hey, if you can slow this thing down, you'd better do it!"

"Okay, but our sensors are out. I can't tell if that Hykzoi ship is still around or not. How close are we?"

"Close enough! I can see cars and little dots where people are in swimming pools."

"Maybe this'll do it." She tried something, but nothing happened.

"Better try something else, Aryl."

She tugged and twisted some more, but the spiraling drop continued.

"I can see people standing around pointing at us. God, I can see their faces. Do something!"

Frantically, Aryl jabbed and poked and hit the controls. Suddenly the ship fluttered, dropped like a stone for a moment, then stopped. Lazily it rocked back and forth not forty feet from the ground.

When Jason opened his eyes again, he saw that they were hanging directly over a parking lot, a parking lot for a school. The playground equipment gave that away. So did all of the faces plastered against the windows on his side of the building.

Guess that's a good way to enliven the school day, he thought crazily. We couldn't finish our spelling test today, Mommy, because a crippled spaceship fell down into our parking lot.

"Well, at least we're not going down anymore," Aryl said in a slightly quavery voice. "But I'm not at all sure how to make us go in any other direction. So many of the controls seem to be fused."

"Aren't there any backups?" Jason asked. Below, a little kid was standing in the playground throwing rocks at them. He waved at the kid just as a woman ran out of the building and snatched him away.

"There ought to be, and I'd know where they were on a Tsorian ship. I can guess, but maybe we'd better lie low a bit in case that Hykzoi is still about."

Lie low, Jason thought, how appropriate. Stretching out on his stomach, he looked out the viewport. Now it seemed the kids were actually evacuating the school. In panicky groups, they were being herded into buses and cars. He felt he should try to send a message that no one was planning to disintegrate the place. Maybe he should write "we come in peace" across the viewport. But why bother? Those kids were getting a day off school. He wouldn't mind going home for a nap himself.

He woke up, astonished that he'd been able to sleep. His cheek felt flat and cold from having been pressed against the viewport. It must have been the lingering effects of that gas. Below him the shadows of the playground and school had lengthened into late afternoon. The parking lot was all but deserted. Except for a military jeep with guys in it.

Startled, he opened his eyes wide and craned around to see more of the scene below. That jeep was being joined by a large truck covered with drab-green canvas. It parked, and soldiers bristling with rifles poured out.

"Aryl," he called, "can rifles do anything to our ship in this condition?"

No answer. He turned to see Aryl slumped in sleep over the console.

Getting up, Jason saw that Rogav and his mother were still out too. But at least their breathing was less ragged. In his sleep, the Tsorian had thrown an arm around Marilyn's waist. Jason figured he should feel indignant, but he couldn't manage it. Just being alive seemed precious enough. He didn't feel like quibbling over the details.

He walked to Aryl and shook her shoulder. "Hey, wake up! There are a bunch of soldiers down there with rifles. Can bullets damage the ship when it's like this?"

"Huh? Oh. Let me see." She ran a hand through her pale tousled hair and stumbled over to the viewport. Kneeling down, she peered out.

"No, I don't think projectile weapons like that could do much, even with our deflectors out. But . . . that now . . . that is something else."

Confused, Jason knelt beside her and followed her gaze

to the far edge of the scene. A large truck had just driven into view, and it carried a very mean-looking piece of artillery. Even as he watched, the truck backed up, pointing the barrel of the gun directly at them.

✹ n i n e t e e n ✹

ARYL LOOKED FROM THE GUN TO JASON, WHOSE PALE COMplexion had become suddenly paler.

"We could write a message on the view screen saying we're not Hykzoi," he suggested.

"No good. These windows are only transparent one way." Standing up, she rushed over to where Rogav was lying and began shaking his shoulders. "Father, wake up, we need you!" She got nothing but a faint groan. "Please wake up. Hey, I've only been bonded a year. I don't know how to fly a Hykzoi ship, not even one that works!"

Finally she stood up again, trying to control her trembling. "It's no use. With althon gas they won't come to till they're ready. I don't even have any medical supplies!"

"Aryl," Jason said from his post by the viewport, "it does really look like they're getting ready to fire that thing."

"All right, all right, I'll try again!" She plunked herself down at the console and began struggling with what she hoped were the right controls. Finally one broke loose, but nothing happened beyond a shower of sparks. She tried another and another. Suddenly the ship quivered and dropped another ten feet.

"Wrong direction!" Jason gasped. "But that did shake up some soldiers."

Angrily Aryl tugged at a frozen lever. "I don't understand why this doesn't . . ." Abruptly their ship shot forward, skimming just above several buildings.

"Look out!" Jason yelled as he glanced toward the forward view screen. A tall apartment building loomed in their path. With a squeal, Aryl yanked at another lever and the ship veered with only seconds to spare.

"Try to get that pink knob to move!" she yelled to Jason, at the same time struggling to steer clear of onrushing buildings. "I think it's the vertical control, and it's jammed."

Jason tugged valiantly at the thing while Aryl kept her fear-widened eyes on the screen. If only she could slow things down a little.

"Here, you steer. I'll see if I can do something about the speed."

"But," Jason protested as he reluctantly grabbed the steering levers, "I don't even have my driver's license yet!"

"You expect your police to stop and arrest you? Just steer."

Jason sank into the seat and looked with horror at the buildings ahead. Jerkily he steered around one, but they seemed to be getting taller in this part of town. Aryl had better move fast.

Throwing herself on her back, Aryl crawled under the control console and tugged at a metal plate. Nothing happened. Then she stuck her claws around the edges and yanked with all her strength. The plate came away, revealing a complex of wires and instruments that only vaguely resembled diagrams she had studied. Still, it was clear that some things were not as they should be. Those fused wires, for instance, or this toggle dangling loose from this connection. Hesitantly she reached in and reconnected the two, her three claws working like delicate instruments. She repeated the process with several other mangled-looking bits. Then she called to her companion.

"There's a green sliding dial on your right. Try moving it now."

At the moment, Jason was absorbed in veering around a multistory parking garage, shooting down a building-lined street, then dodging a church spire. But when they sailed over a park and ornamental lake, he had a chance to locate the green dial and slide it an experimental inch.

Abruptly they plumeted downward. Aryl rolled out from under the panels to see the view screen darkened with green water and a few flashes that might have been terrified fish. "Other way!"

Already Jason was ramming the dial in the other direction. They erupted in a cloud of spray and continued shooting skyward.

Aryl tried not to giggle, not knowing how sensitive humans were to being laughed at. Then she knew she needn't have worried.

Jason's tense shoulders relaxed with spasms of laughter. "Good thing the driving examiner isn't along on this trip. He might ask me to parallel park on Main Street."

"No," she said between laughing gasps, "he'd have his hands clamped over his eyes all the way."

Aryl went back to tugging at the pink control, which suddenly moved fairly easily. Their speed immediately slowed. "Well, I got the acceleration and vertical controls reversed, but at least they both work now."

"So where do we go?" Jason said, finally recovering himself.

"Well, I know the coordinates Father transmitted, but we don't know if any Tsorians ever received them."

"So if that radio thing still works, we'll have to start broadcasting again."

"But I don't know the code. It's a matter of very subtle inflection."

"Hmm. And if you broadcast in straight Tsorian, the Hykzoi are sure to pick it up and meet us there."

"Should we try English?" Aryl suggested.

"Better not. That slime Jerry Barns got through to the Hykzoi in English. They must have done at least that much homework before invading this place."

"Right." She frowned a moment then looked speculatively at Jason. "But a number of our people learned other Earth languages besides the official one. Some collect languages as a hobby, to pass the time on different assignments. Do you know any?"

"Other languages?" Jason paled again, then blushed. Aryl marveled at the versatility of his complexion. "Well, I . . . er . . . I've studied a little Spanish in school. But I'm only in the second year. Señora Cortez thinks I really don't 'apply' myself. She's right."

Aryl grinned. "Well, now's your chance. I'll tell you what to say, and you translate it into Spanish."

"But my grammar's awful! And I don't have much vocabulary."

"Nobody's going to grade you on it! All we need is something that no Hykzoi is likely to know and some Tsorian might."

Jason turned to the communication console. "I just hope Señora Cortez isn't listening on a CB," he muttered.

Aryl outlined the basic message, and Jason, with much grumbling, finally came up with a translation and started

172

repeating it into the communicator. Pretty soon he seemed to have slipped into a confident rhythm, and Aryl turned her attention to the two adults still lying on the deck. The human was whimpering slightly and seemed to be coming out of it. Aryl waved Jason back to his broadcasting and said she'd take care of them.

Gently she raised Marilyn's head onto her lap and began rubbing her temples. She wasn't sure this helped with humans, but it probably wouldn't hurt. Now that she really looked at her, Aryl had to admit this woman was not unattractive. Her skin, of course, was much too soft and the wrong shade. And her nose was too short for beauty. But her hair, unorthodox color that it might me, was striking, almost the color of sunsets around here. And politics aside, she seemed a nice enough person, and certainly close to her son, even without bonding. Aryl sighed. She really couldn't blame her father . . .

Her thoughts were interrupted by a new voice, bursting from the communicator. *"Buenos dias, señor,"* said an obviously Tsorian voice. Haltingly it continued, leaving Aryl furious that she couldn't understand. As soon as the voice signed off, she blurted out, "What did he say?"

"He said they're coming. Loosely translated, that is. His accent was even worse than mine."

"Who is coming?" a weak voice asked.

Aryl looked down into Marilyn's open blue eyes. "How are you feeling?" she asked anxiously.

"I have a splitting headache. I kept dreaming I was back in school and Jason was trying to teach me Spanish. Who did you say was coming?" She struggled to sit up. "Where's Rogav?"

"Here," a hoarse voice said beside them. "Wishing I

weren't. My head's exploding. But to repeat the question, who is coming?"

"Your people are, sir," Jason answered. "They just replied that they'll meet us at the coordinates you set."

Rogav looked surprised. "They responded to the broadcast I sent?"

Aryl smiled. "No, to the one Jason sent. He's been broadcasting in Spanish, figuring no Hykzoi would know it."

"Good work, Jason," Rogav said, cautiously sitting up. "If you were part of our forces, I'd give you some sort of commendation."

Aryl watched a blush steal over Jason's face again. She wondered whether it was pride, embarrassment, or a confusing mix of both. She knew that last well enough.

Helping the other two into seats, Aryl and Jason briefly described their difficulties with the Hykzoi, the U.S. Army, and the ship's controls. After a while, Rogav commented, "That phrase was very apt. 'Out of the frying pan, into the fire.' Have I got it right now?"

"Yes," Marilyn said distractedly, "and it *is* apt since there're some more of those red ships coming."

Immediately they all crowded around the floor viewport to watch a large cluster of red rings rising toward them from the night-darkened planet. Aryl's heart sank. "Did they know Spanish after all?"

"I think not," Rogav said, hurrying back to the control console. "They've probably been tracking this ship since it cleared the planet's surface. You said our external sensors are out?"

"None are registering. We didn't try the weapons again."

"Well, if they work, we can go down fighting, but with

no deflectors the battle won't last long. Are we near those rescue coordinates yet?"

"Probably," Jason said. "But we weren't too sure about the setting. Hey, look!"

Quickly Aryl joined him at the front view screen. For a flashing moment she felt as if she were back on her nursery world, swimming in a quiet lagoon and looking up at the sun glinting on the surface. She'd push off and rise through a shoal of glittering blue fish. There they were, blue triangular lights, a shoal of them! Coming closer and closer.

"The Fleet," Rogav sighed. "Or what's left of it."

When they turned their attention back to the bottom screen, however, it was clear that the Hykzoi weren't giving up their quarry without a fight. Aryl saw an energy bolt rising toward them almost in slow motion. In moments, red light had engulfed them.

She huddled on the lurching deck, arms thrown over her head. Incongruously she thought of the times as a little girl when she'd run inside at every meteor shower, fearfully wrapping herself in her sleeping mat. She longed for that mat now, something protective and safe.

Someone was huddling close beside her, but there was nothing to see besides bursts of red and blue. She could feel whimpering in her throat, but the only sounds were the shrieking explosions.

Aryl awoke to utter silence. And darkness. She was a jettisoned body, floating alone in space, drifting forever between the stars. Then she knew she must be alive. Her lungs were laboring to draw in thin, cold air. It was the ship that was floating derelict in space. And the silence was not total. Somewhere there was breathing other than her own.

But there was no mechanical noise. The ship sounded dead. It felt dead. It had none of that almost undetectable sense of working engines and life-support systems. In a few minutes the air would be gone, and they would die with the ship.

"Aryl?" Her father's voice came from above her. Reaching up, she gripped his hand, then swayed to her feet as Rogav held her to him, fighting back the growing cold.

From near her feet came another tremulous voice. "Mom, where are you? Are we still alive?"

"Here I am, Jason." There was a shuffling noise, and Aryl knew Marilyn had made her way to her son.

Rogav spoke quietly into the dark and spreading cold. "We're all alive for the moment. But if there aren't any Tsorians left to retrieve us . . ."

Nobody finished the sentence. The air was thin now and cut Aryl's throat like cold knives. But her eyes were getting used to the darkness. She could make out the huddled forms of Jason and his mother.

Her heart tightened. She and her father could expect a death like this. But Jason . . . it was sad he had to die not even touching his own world. Maybe this battle *was* his, but he'd hardly asked for it.

Pulling herself away from her father, she stepped toward the two natives. She could see them better now. Tears glistened in the eyes of the woman, but Jason's eyes were turned toward hers.

In fact, she could see them *surprisingly* well. At the same moment, all four looked to the forward view screen and on numbed feet stumbled toward it. Luminous, star-flecked space was taking on a definite blue cast. In moments, the edge of a glowing blue ship lowered into view. Their own ship gave a convulsive shudder.

"An energy lock," Rogav whispered hoarsely. "They're pulling us in."

By the time they had clanked against the hull of the other ship, the air Aryl was gasping seemed almost too thin and cold to fight for. Dizzily she and her father struggled to hold up the two natives. Jason's breathing was shallow and ragged as he sagged against her. The blue light now flooding the cabin showed his eyes dazed and filmy looking. "Don't give up now," she gasped. Then her knees buckled, and they slid in a heap to the floor, joined moments later by the other two.

Blue light was replaced with clear. There was more thumping and clanging. They must be inside the other ship, she thought dully. But could anyone get to them? Could this hatch even be opened with their own power out?

The answer came in a wondrous burst of light and air, rich breathable air. The hatch on the floor yawned open, and in seconds black-uniformed Tsorians were scrambling in and pulling the four of them out.

Soon she was standing on a new, familiar-feeling deck. Doctors fussed about them with injections and monitors, but the air was all she needed. She took great deep breaths and joyously hugged the others. Her pride in them all seemed every bit as heady as the new oxygen in her blood.

Then she struggled to recover some dignity as officers came up to them, saluting her father and expressing their delight at having him back. Aryl scanned the faces and suddenly saw someone standing shyly back, a radiant smile on his usually dour face. Theelk. She shot him an answering grin. If anyone deserved to have survived, deserved to have seen the return of their Commander, it was First Adjutant Theelk.

Soon the four of them were ushered out of the hold and into lift tubes, which brought them to the top of the command bridge. The dome arching overhead was transparent, showing the sparse canopy of stars spread in patterns Aryl was beginning to recognize. To one side spread the rim of a blue-green planet.

As disheveled and battered as the Fleet Commander was, his arrival brought unrestrained cheering from the crew ranged below. At last Rogav raised an answering salute and launched into a short, impromptu speech.

Marilyn was struggling to follow the Tsorian words, but Jason simply looked around wide-eyed. His gaze lingered longest on the planet glowing warmly beneath him. Aryl saw him swallow hard, and she reached to squeeze his hand.

"Father thanked them for the rescue," she whispered, as translation, "and then he told them about you and your mother, how you risked your lives for us and showed him how important your people and your world can be to the Empire."

When the cheers rose anew, Rogav gently pulled the other three forward to receive them with him. Aryl watched Jason's face turn as red as a Hykzoi ship, though he smiled and nodded shyly.

Aryl's amusement bubbled into pride. This alien wasn't all that bad. In fact, he wasn't really all that alien. Neither was his world. Looking at her father, she was suddenly very glad he had brought them here. And if this was any example, her career might not be orthodox, but it certainly wouldn't be boring.

❧ t w e n t y ❧

JASON STARED OUT AT THE WILDLY ALIEN LANDSCAPE. THE sun had just set, small and angry, behind the barren red horizon. But now, with the sun gone, the planet's thin atmosphere had given up all pretense of making a sky. The stars, which had peered through even in daylight, had now taken over. Their patterns were familiar, but not their unblinking intensity. And among them, glowing like a blue sapphire over the western horizon, hung the evening star. The planet Earth.

He shifted his eyes away. It was hard to believe that that distant glimmer was really home, even though he had watched it shrink to this size from a great glowing sphere. But then, everything seemed hard to believe lately. So much had happened.

The ship that had rescued them had seemed huge. It had until the Tsorian flagship had come into view, dwarfing everything, like an aircraft carrier beside tugboats. And after a surprisingly painful parting, Fleet Commander Rogav Jy and his bond-daughter had transferred to that colossus. They and the remaining fleet had gone off to resume the battle, while Jason and his mother, along with several damaged ships, had been sent to the maintenance base on Mars.

Mars. Again he looked at the cold, alien landscape and the equally alien towers and domes of the Tsorian base. Mars. His father and the Resisters would probably have said that this too had been taken from them. For eons humans had dreamed of walking on this planet, of making it their own. And now their dreams had been stolen. But maybe, Jason thought suddenly, maybe they just hadn't been dreaming big enough. They'd written stories and imagined futures, but they hadn't really let their imaginations loose on *all* the possibilities.

Jason was jarred from his thoughts by the sound of his name. He looked down the spiraling ramp that led into the clear-walled body of the Tsorian base. He and his mother had been given free run of the place and had spent their days here exploring—and waiting. Again his name was called, and there was something in the tone of his mother's voice that suggested that, one way or another, their waiting was over.

"Here. Up here."

Marilyn moved quickly up the ramp, auburn hair bouncing lightly in the low gravity. "I should have guessed I'd find you in the observation tower. You gravitate here just the way you used to go to Indian Rock."

"Guess it's my kind of place. You have some news?"

"Yes." She paused. "There's been a decisive battle. A very, very costly one. But the Hykzoi, the remaining ones, have retreated."

"And . . . and the Tsorian flagship?"

She smiled. "That's where the message came from. It survived."

For a moment, their smiles matched. "And," she continued, "Rogav . . . Commander Rogav said that they would be returning to this base for a while. He will be making a report to the Emperor, and his first recommendation will be changing our planet's status from a military outpost to a full part of their empire."

Her expression turned wistful, and she shook her head. "So I guess it really hasn't been in vain, any of it. Though it's funny, this is hardly what we once would have wanted—if we ever could have said exactly what that was."

"Maybe we just wanted a chance to make our own future."

Suddenly his mother hugged him. "Jason, I think that may be what we have." She turned and hurried down the ramp back to the communications room.

Jason started to follow, then paused. With a surge of confidence he looked back at the familiar sky. No, it hadn't been in vain. His father, Ricky Jensen, Professor Ackerman, all of them. In a strange way, they had won after all. They had won back the stars.

He turned and walked down the ramp.

about the author

Pamela Service grew up in Berkeley, California. She received a bachelor's degree in political science from the University of California and a master's degree in African prehistory from the University of London. While living in England, she and her husband spent free time on political campaigns, touring ancient sites, and digging in excavations in Britain and the Sudan.

Now settled in Bloomington, Indiana with her husband and daughter, Ms. Service is curator of the county historical museum and a member of the Bloomington City Council.

PAMELA SERVICE'S

Fantasy Books
for
Young Adults